STREETWISE

A brutal killing in a New York taxi – a close friend arrested for the murder...

Ex-cop Joseph Soyinka made many enemies fighting corruption but refused to be intimidated – until his wife was killed and his life destroyed. Now he lives with his young son in the anonymous safety of New York City. By day he drives a yellow cab. By night he tries to forget about the past. Joseph knows his friend Cyrus is not a murderer, but he *is* involved in something – and he's in way over his head. The only way to find the real killer is to take Cyrus's place in a deadly game.

STREETWISE

STREETWISE

by

Chris Freeman

Dales Large Print Books
Long Preston, North Yorkshire,
BD23 4ND, England.

British Library Cataloguing in Publication Data.

Freeman, Chris
    Streetwise.

    A catalogue record of this book is
    available from the British Library

    ISBN   978-1-84262-737-2 pbk

First published in Great Britain in 2008 by
Black Star Crime

Copyright © Working Partners 2008

Cover illustration © Michael Manzarero by arrangement with
Arcangel Images

The moral right of the author has been asserted

Published in Large Print 2010 by arrangement with
Harlequin Enterprises II B.V./S. à.r.l.,

Dales Large Print is an imprint of Library Magna Books Ltd.

Printed and bound in Great Britain by
T.J. (International) Ltd., Cornwall, PL28 8RW

With special thanks to Howard Linskey
For Erin and Alison

'*The Bronx?*
No thonks,'
–Ogden Nash, *The New Yorker*

1

Joseph Soyinka should have known better than to pick an argument with a stranger. One minute you are driving around minding your own business, the next thing you are staring down the barrel of a gun. That's how easy it was to get yourself killed in the South Bronx.

His day had started promisingly enough, as had his ancient Crown Victoria cab, which uncharacteristically purred into life that morning on the first flick of its ignition despite the biting cold at the onset of a New York winter. Then Yomi managed to be ready for school on time, which enabled his father to hit the road early and pickup a business type in a cheap suit as he emerged from his hotel. The trip to La Guardia had been a good fare, delivering a solid tip from the guy who was happy to drop Joseph a little extra green, as long as it was on the receipt and his company was paying. The traffic kept moving and he was soon off the Cross Bronx Expressway and back into the tenements, his home patch. For the rest of the morning and well into the afternoon the fares were steady and he kept on earning.

Even the lights seemed to turn green as he reached them. So how had it suddenly gone so badly wrong?

Joseph had spotted his next fare hailing a cab some way up the street, another businessman in a dark suit and tie, briefcase in hand. Joseph wondered who he had come to see in the South Bronx dressed like that. It had to be another real-estate deal. He pressed down on the accelerator, eager to get the job, but at the last moment an unmarked car pulled in sharply from the opposite side of the road to steal his fare.

'Son of a bitch,' he said aloud, another Americanism he'd picked up lately, and he slammed on the brakes as the beat-up Toyota cut him up, coming way too close to the front fender for comfort.

The businessman climbed in to the unlicensed cab and that would have been the end of it, if it hadn't been for the hot-headed Hispanic guy at the wheel. He'd noticed Joseph's anger and wound down the window, his face contorted with rage. 'What's your fucking problem?' he snarled, before adding an uncomplimentary reference to Joseph's black skin.

Joseph Soyinka had spent a year keeping his nose clean, his mouth shut and his temper at bay. He knew there was little to be gained from a stand-up row in the middle of the street with a man who was barely one step up from a petty criminal, stealing the fares from guys who drove legitimate vehicles and paid for the medallion that hung from their dashboard. Ninety-nine times out of a hundred, Joseph would have let it go without a word, but maybe it was the racial slur, or perhaps it was just one injustice too many, because suddenly he found himself winding down his window.

The cold winter air pinched Joseph's face as he called out, 'I'm trying to earn a living here and you just stole my fare.'

The Hispanic seemed a little stunned that anyone would talk back to him and paused momentarily as if he was sizing up an opponent. Joseph was tall and muscular and he sat high in the cab's front seat. His jet-black hair made him look younger than his forty years and he had the bearing of a man not easily pushed around. Back in Lagos, women had liked him and men had not taken him lightly. In America, where every-one wants to play the gangster, it was a little different. The Hispanic finally settled on 'Fuck you!' then he regained his composure and asked, 'Wanna see something else I stole?' and that's when the gun came out.

The Hispanic had looked from right to left before he pulled the .38, but when he was sure nobody, including his startled pass-enger, could see what he was carrying, he held it up for Joseph to take a good look at.

Though he kept the gun inside the car and pressed it close to his chest, it was pointed straight at Joseph. A look of triumphant glee spread across the guy's unwashed and stubbly face.

Joseph didn't carry a piece, hadn't done so since he left Nigeria in such a hurry barely a year ago. There was nothing he could do. 'Want a closer look asshole?' said the Hispanic, and for a moment Joseph was filled not with fear but an impotent fury. He wanted to get out of his cab, grab the gun and knock some sense into this pretend hard man with it. If the gun went off and took him out before he reached the grinning idiot then fine, all his problems would be over at a stroke. Immediately though he thought of his son and his fury was swiftly replaced by shame. How would Yomi feel if he learned that his father had been gunned down in a stupid row over a twenty-dollar cab fare? Joseph told himself his son had to come first over everything, particularly his father's stupid pride.

Glancing down at the .38 in the guy's hand, Joseph spoke quietly and dismissively. 'Big man with your little gun.'

'What you say?' demanded the Hispanic, who knew he had been insulted but wasn't quite sure how.

It was too late. Joseph had already wound the window back up and he was on his way.

The last thing he noticed of the other car was the nervous face of the businessman in the back. Dumb-ass suit now knew the risk he was taking climbing into an unlicensed cab, thought Joseph. He could end up in the projects standing there in his underwear. If he was lucky.

Ten blocks away and Joseph was still brooding about the guy with the gun when his mobile started to trill. It was Cyrus sounding agitated, but there was always drama in Cyrus's life.

'Joseph, it's me,' he said in that unmistakeably deep voice of his, before unnecessarily adding, 'Cyrus. I need to talk to you, my friend, better sooner than later. Can you come by? I got a drop-off near the Impala later.'

Joseph sighed. It's not that he didn't like Cyrus, who was truly one of life's good guys, but he didn't really have time for this. 'That's not going to be easy, Cyrus. I've not got a free hour today, believe me, not one.'

There was silence on the end of the line then Cyrus said simply, 'Got to see you somehow, Joseph.'

For a moment he thought about refusing, but then Joseph wondered if his friend might really be in trouble. He and Cyrus went way back to the mother country and beyond, into that foreign land of a distant, half-remembered childhood in Nigeria

15

together. Joseph owed him, big time. If it weren't for Cyrus he wouldn't be driving this cab. He might not be working for Donald Trump, but the cab fares put food on the table and a roof over their heads. No one else except Cyrus had given a shit when Joseph arrived in the land of the free, with just his son and a couple of suitcases. Back then, Joseph had no future to speak of and a past that still kept him awake every night, even now. Cyrus had taken them both in until they could find a low-rate apartment of their own, then he got Joseph a job at the same cab company as him. Joseph didn't like to think where he would be right now if it weren't for that. He pulled the cab over at the side of the road so he could speak to his friend without distraction.

'Is it important?' asked Joseph.

'Yeah, man.' Cyrus's deep voice was filled with melancholy.

'Okay, okay,' Joseph relented. 'I'll see if I can get to you at the Impala later, might take me a while though.'

'I'm not going anywhere.' And he could hear the relief in Cyrus's voice.

Just then there was a loud rap on the side window. Joseph jerked his head towards the rear seat and she climbed in. His passenger was a black woman in her early thirties, neatly dressed and polite, which was a big improvement on his usual fares. Joseph was no longer sure who were the worst; the lowlifes who didn't know any better than to call him 'bro' or 'my nigga,' like they'd just stepped off a shoot for a gangsta-rap video, or the business types. When the guys in suits saw the name Joseph Soyinka on the dashboard ID they immediately treated him like he was none too clever. His last pick-up had mouthed the word 'Air-port' exaggeratedly at him as if he were deaf.

This lady was different. She talked in sentences and added the word "please" at the end. Rare indeed, which was why Joseph was taken aback when he heard her destination was St Mary's, the rehab clinic. She didn't look like a junkie to Joseph but then that was none of his business. At least the place wasn't too far from the Impala. Maybe he could drop by there afterwards.

All of a sudden the lights were against him and Joseph was crawling along, bumper to bumper. Apartment blocks loomed above them on either side, red bricks turned to a dark grey from decades of smog and exhaust fumes. Long, metal fire escapes, like the ones he'd seen in the movies back in Lagos, hung down from the roofs almost to street level, but you had to drag them the last floor, as if they didn't actually want to touch the South Bronx unless they really had to.

The lady leaned forwards then and tutted to herself. 'It's always the way when I got to get to work.'

'You a nurse?' asked Joseph.

'Yep, work at the clinic and I get to do the school visits, too. I gotta persuade the kids not to do drugs.' And she sighed. 'I don't s'pose they listen much at their age, you know kids, but I tell 'em anyways. You got any?' she asked brightly. 'Kids, I mean, not drugs.'

Joseph laughed. 'A boy.'

'How old's he?'

'Eleven.'

'That's nice. You close or is he all "get the hell out of my room, dad"?'

'No, he's not like that. We're close.' Over his shoulder he passed her a picture of Yomi standing proudly with his dad outside the Yankee stadium.

'Oh, he's a handsome young man. Takes after his momma I guess?' She was teasing him and Joseph laughed easily along with her, even though she had made him think of Apara.

'Yes, he takes after his mother.'

'And what does she do?'

Joseph fell silent. He wasn't sure why he couldn't lie and say she's a waitress, a schoolteacher or a nurse even, like the kind lady in the back of his cab. It would be so much easier.

'I don't mean to...' she began.

'No, it's okay, it's just...'

'That's alright, honey, it's none of my business, but you give that boy a hug for me when you see him next and you tell him his aunt Josephine said to say no to drugs, period.'

'Your name is Josephine?'

'Uh-huh.'

'I'm Joseph.'

'Well isn't that something, you and me is two sides of the same coin, Joseph.' She looked out of the window again. 'Looks like we ain't moving.'

'It's usually okay this time of day,' said Joseph. 'Something's up.' There was more to this than the normal grind. Something pretty bad had to have happened up ahead. It looked more serious than a red-light jumper mowing down a pedestrian. Joseph switched on the radio, turning the volume down so he could ignore the local shock-jock. They were stuck right by an old tenement that seemed to have taken in washing for the whole of the South Bronx. Every balcony had something white draped from it.

'Must be a good drying day,' said Josephine.

'It looks to me like the whole building gave up this morning and surrendered,' said Joseph, and his passenger was still laughing at this when a new presenter came on the radio and Joseph turned up the volume.

This voice was older, more authoritative. 'We have breaking news just coming in of a shooting in Highbridge. Details are sketchy, but an eyewitness reports that a Crown Victoria taxi has been shot up by the side of the road. Police are at the scene and there is believed to have been at least one fatality. Traffic is backed up right along the main drag so you'll want to find an alternate route. More on that shooting as soon as we get it.'

'I hate to say it, honey, but it looks like you gonna be here for a while,' said Josephine and she pushed some money through the slot. 'I'd better walk the rest of the way. Take care of yourself, you hear.'

'Thanks. You, too,' said Joseph, but his mind was elsewhere. A cab involved in a shooting just a few blocks from the Impala? Cyrus?

He found Cyrus's number on his cell phone and dialled, then listened with mounting apprehension while it rang and rang. Eventually, an emotionless female voice asked him to be patient because the person he wanted was unavailable, but he was about to be transferred to their voice mail. Joseph hung up. Why was Cyrus not picking up his damn phone, unless he was in that wreck? Joseph told himself to stay calm.

Cyrus could easily be on another call or just driving between the old tenements where it was hard to get a signal. Even so, Joseph made a decision. He sounded his horn at the guy in front, then gestured for him to pull forwards a couple of yards so he could take the next left-hand turn. It was little more than an alley, but he knew every rat-run around here. Joseph was gambling he could make a horseshoe and bypass the incident up ahead. As he drove he couldn't take his mind from the shooting. That same morning, someone had pulled a gun on Joseph for no good reason, but he had been the fortunate one. Half an hour and just a few blocks away in the same city, someone else had not been so lucky. He prayed it wasn't his friend. Joseph told himself it could have been anybody in a city this size but, try as he might, he couldn't shake a growing sense of foreboding.

Anxious to reach the scene of the shooting, Joseph steered the cab expertly through the side streets at speed, taking care to avoid pedestrians as he turned the car through some tight bends. The last one brought him back onto the road he'd just left, emerging through a gap between two liquor stores, only to find he'd not quite made it. In fact, he was slap bang in the middle of things by the look of the ambulance nearby, its light flashing insistently at passersby.

Traffic was backed up bumper to bumper so tight he couldn't even leave the side street. The street was one-way so he'd be taking a big chance if he reversed back down it, but that might be his only option. Joseph decided to get out and take a look first, partly to see if the police were preoccupied enough for him to risk a little traffic violation, but mostly he was propelled by an old instinct. The first thing he noticed was the patience of the other drivers. No one was beeping a horn or leaning from a window to shout a complaint about the delay, and he could see why. The radio reports were accurate. Two paramedics were carrying a stretcher back to the ambulance, but they were in no kind of hurry.

The body was covered from head to toe by a long, green sheet tucked neatly in at the sides, so there was no telling the age, description or even the sex of the victim. If this was a movie, thought Joseph, then a hand would fall out from under the sheet, to hang down off the stretcher and give a clue. But it wasn't a movie, and the paramedics were far too professional to let that happen. Instead the corpse was wrapped up all neat and tidy, like a birthday present.

Joseph took a few steps closer and it was clear that the incident had only just occurred. The police were starting to tape off the area, struggling to keep back an inquisitive crowd. As he came nearer, Joseph spotted the vehicle, which had gone right off the road and into some railings, but not before it hit a streetlamp along the way. The lamp at the top of the pole was almost bent double, hanging down towards the ground like a weeping willow.

The police were woefully undermanned for the task of keeping the public at bay and Joseph took advantage. He felt compelled to draw nearer. What if it were his friend's cab? What if it was Cyrus lying dead on the stretcher? He was advancing towards the front of the car, but it was the wrong angle for him to make out the registration as the plate was buried in the railings. He couldn't identify the cab or its owner, but he could make out the telltale cracks in the front windshield that could only have been caused by a bullet. They were long, white and jagged, spread right out across the glass, like a giant spider's web covered in dew. Joseph pushed his way through the gathering crowd of onlookers until he could see the rear windshield. To an innocent observer it might look as if something had exploded inside the vehicle, but Joseph knew that the debris on the rear window of the old cab was blood and brain matter, propelled onto it by the force of a head-shot exit wound.

Joseph had seen far worse in his time, but

there was something about the positioning of the damaged car, its broken windshield and the lurid blood stains that made his heart suddenly start to pound and the blood go to his head in a rush. The crowd was thickening around him, they were pushing and shoving, eager to catch a glimpse of the scene, but Joseph was already miles from there, remembering another day, another murder.

That time it had been a white Mercedes, badly dented by its impact with the oil palm trees, and there was broken glass on the ground all around it. The driver had struggled desperately to escape from the men who had run him off the road but they had been too quick and the bullets had taken him in the chest, shoulder and head as soon as he emerged from the car. The dead man's leg had become caught in his seat belt as he fell, and he had landed face first on the bone-dry African soil. An hour later, Joseph had peered down at the broken body knowing he had lost.

'Well, sir,' said Sergeant Aweto, as he appeared at Joseph's shoulder and recognised the murdered man. 'Looks like it's over.'

'Yes,' said Joseph. 'It is.' And it was all over. Back then, Aweto had no idea how right he had been.

2

'Hey, Move along!'

An angry overweight cop was waving at pedestrians, trying to clear them from the scene. 'Get outta here!' he ordered, but they didn't seem to want to move or maybe they just couldn't hear him now that they were up so close to an actual murder scene.

It had only taken a few curious bystanders to break ranks and walk to the cab and all of a sudden there were people everywhere, like the others didn't want to miss out on something this juicy. It was as if they had all suddenly become extras on their favourite cop show.

The fat cop was acting like he had heartburn and the crowd was moving with as much cooperation as sheep, parting when he moved amongst them only to reform again behind him to gaze at the wreck. Meanwhile Joseph, standing off to one side, took advantage of the cop's preoccupation to survey the crime scene. There was no sign of the driver or his passenger, which meant one of them was in the ambulance, but which one? The shot had gone through the front windshield so Joseph had to assume the driver was the target, but the blood and brains was plastered all over the back window, so he couldn't be sure who had taken the bullet.

A young cop joined his fat friend and was mimicking the veteran, trying to look more world weary than it was possible to be at his age, as he herded onlookers back towards the imaginary perimeter they were trying to establish.

'I drive a cab,' said Joseph to the younger one. 'Liable to know that driver. He okay?' Joseph knew knowledge was power and most cops, particularly rookies, like to show they know more than you do. It makes them feel important.

'Minor injuries,' growled the rookie. 'As for the passenger, don't ask.'

Joseph didn't have to. The ambulance had driven away silently, in no particular rush to reach the hospital morgue. From here, Joseph could finally make out the cab's rear licence plate. To his immense relief, he did not recognise the number. Whoever was driving that cab, it wasn't Cyrus.

He wondered who the driver had been and immediately thought about the unfortunate passenger. Hail a cab in this city and the next thing you know you get a bullet in the brain because someone has a beef with your driver, a guy you never even met before. That's the worst luck imaginable, thought

Joseph. He was about to ask another question when the fat cop pushed passed the young one and shouted, 'I ain't telling you again!' He was right in Joseph's face, pressing a baton into his chest with both hands so hard that Joseph almost toppled over.

Joseph held up a placatory hand and said, 'Okay, okay.' Then the fat cop went off to ruin somebody else's day. Joseph walked back to his cab, fully intending to get as far away from the NYPD as possible, but he had the crime scene playing on his mind now. There was no sign of another car involved in the crash, no blown-out tyres or debris to explain why it had come off the road, so it had to have been the shot through the front windshield that had caused the driver to swerve into the lamp post.

When Joseph reached the cab, the traffic hadn't budged an inch. He thought what the hell and backed the cab up, putting two wheels and half the car up on the kerb, so another driver could get by him if he needed to. He reached into the glove compartment and fished out his battered old Nikon. Joseph walked swiftly towards the wrecked cab and fired off a couple of quick shots before he heard the fat cop's voice boom out again, 'Hey! What d'ya think...' But he didn't catch the last words for he was already gone, weaving his way back through the crowd.

There was a Chinese take-out next to one of the liquor stores and, when he was sure the fat cop was not following him, Joseph ducked in through the front door. He knew he had no time to cook anything now and Yomi wouldn't mind. In fact he'd think it was a treat to eat Chinese food during the week, instead of his dad's awful cooking. The take-out looked right onto the road and the wrecked cab could still be seen through its window now the crowd had been pushed back.

They were doing more business than usual because of the traffic backing up and it was hot and humid from all the cooking going on out back. Joseph joined a queue just inside the front door. He could see the frantic activity as steam rose from hissing pans and food was tossed into the air by two young oriental chefs dressed in white. The owner was making his way down the queue, passing orders back to two silent girls who could be his daughters, wisecracking his way along the line.

'Oh, it's Russell Crowe!' he chirped to a guy who had only the vaguest possible resemblance to the film star. 'How you doing, Russell? We like you in *Gladiator* very much.' The guy acted embarrassed, but he loved it really and so did his girlfriend. Before you could say Sweet 'n' Sour, the owner got their order back to the counter and he reached Joseph. 'Mr Denzel Washington!' he called. 'Such an honour. How's it hanging, Denzel?'

'Oh, you know,' deadpanned Joseph. 'Movie business sucks.'

Everybody laughed at this, even though it wasn't much of a joke. It was as if closeness to death had made them all stop stressing about the little things for once.

Unhappy at being upstaged, the Russell Crowe not-so-look-a-like interrupted, 'Anyone know where I can get a cab round here?' he said, expecting a big laugh.

That ought to kill it, thought Joseph and, sure enough, there wasn't a murmur in reply. The girlfriend started looking at her shoes.

'Terrible thing,' said the owner and he took another look at the cab. 'Who'd do something like that?' he asked no one in particular. 'Plenty of people I guess,' he concluded glumly.

'You see what happened?' Joseph asked, under the guise of conversation.

'See it, no,' said the owner. 'We hear it, sure! Even outback sweeping up, I hear it. Big bang and I mean big, like a firecracker, then the tyres screech-screech then a smash. I go out there, make the girls stay inside. I don't get too close though,' he grimaced and lowered his voice to keep it from his

29

girls, 'not when I see the blood all over the back windshield. Call the cops instead, let them deal with it.'

Before too long, Joseph got his chow mein and Kung-po chicken. The police had more to worry about, so Joseph risked reversing the cab, his food balanced carefully on the passenger seat beside him. It was only when he reached the bottom of the street that he remembered his meeting with Cyrus. What if it *had* been his friend driving that cab? Maybe he should make that detour.

'Joseph man, take the weight off your feet,' ordered Cyrus. He extended a spidery leg and pushed the stool he had been saving across the floor with his foot. 'Want a Rooibos?'

'Great,' answered Joseph. Cyrus knew he preferred the honey-flavoured tea to anything else when he was driving. A real drink could wait until his neighbour Eddie called by later.

As usual the Impala was busy, filled with homesick customers looking for their own slice of West Africa in the Big Apple. Joseph watched as waitresses brought out plates of Suya, plantain and yam. He recognised a number of drivers from their cab firm – which was only two doors down – who nodded at the two men before returning to

30

their food. This was the place Cyrus had taken Joseph when the homesickness first hit him, for a plate of beef Suya and a glass of palm wine.

'Fares are slow these days,' said Cyrus. 'Cold weather's coming in. People are staying at home.'

There was a preoccupation in Cyrus's tone as if he wanted to come to the matter in hand but didn't know how to get there. Joseph waited till the tea arrived, then he asked Cyrus if he had heard about the shooting. Cyrus's smile vanished.

'It's all anyone is talking about. They are saying it was the passenger, a young woman, who was killed.' His tone was incredulous, as if he couldn't imagine why anyone would commit such an evil act. That was Cyrus's trouble, thought Joseph. He was a little too innocent for this world.

'Really?'

'That's what they say, but nobody seems to know who was driving that cab.'

'Not one of our guys then?'

Cyrus shrugged. 'No. But it's a bad business. The same thing has happened before.'

'What do you mean?'

'People taking pot shots at drivers. A few months after I arrived here, cab drivers started dying. Everybody was scared. It was a terrible time.'

Joseph could tell his friend was rattled by

the memory and he decided to change the subject. 'Anyway, what's up, Cyrus? You in some kind of trouble?'

Cyrus seemed taken aback by the directness of Joseph's question. He paused for a moment before finally offering, 'Maybe.' He said it cautiously, waiting for a reaction, but Joseph was not about to let his friend off the hook that easily. He let the silence between them become a void until Cyrus felt compelled to fill it. He leaned forwards confidentially.

'I met this fellow.' He said it softly, in that earnest, peculiarly formal English he reverted to when he was explaining something. It made him sound part Eddie Murphy, part Sherlock Holmes. Who else but Cyrus would use the word fellow to describe anybody these days. 'One of the guys introduced me to him.' Joseph noticed Cyrus did not name the driver who had made the introduction. 'This fellow said he knew I needed money and that maybe he could help me to earn some extra.' And how did he know that? thought Joseph. Cyrus was never discreet, always too keen to tell his problems to anyone who would listen – small wonder that gangsters approached him with dangerous propositions. Joseph almost didn't need to hear the rest. He had practically guessed it already.

'He needed delivery drivers, good people,

men he could trust.' Joseph winced and his friend must have seen the disappointment in his face. 'Joseph. I know. I have been a terrible fool.' Cyrus halted then, reluctant to finish the tale.

'Go on.'

'He asked me to deliver some packages for him. I didn't know what they were. He told me not to look inside, so I didn't. He paid well, very well.'

'You didn't know what they were,' coaxed Joseph, 'but you could have guessed.' Cyrus looked truly ashamed then. 'From the money he gave you, you could have guessed.'

'Yes,' Cyrus finally admitted, 'I could have guessed. It was too much money for just a delivery.'

Joseph lowered his voice, 'Drugs?'

Cyrus nodded grimly.

'Oh, Cyrus, what have you done?'

'I know, I thought maybe I could do this thing but it wouldn't touch me, do you understand?'

Frowning, Joseph said, 'no,' and meant it.

'I told myself I was not selling these drugs, only delivering for the men who sold them and that somehow this was not the same. I convinced myself the people who used the drugs were fools who would buy them anyway, whether I was involved or not. They were lost already so I might as well make some money. Joseph, I was desperate.'

The excuse of every criminal down through the ages, thought Joseph, and he saw Cyrus in a new light. 'But it wasn't that simple, was it?' he asked.

'No,' and it was as if he had stuck a knife into his friend. 'Have you seen these people? I mean really seen them, up close, the way they live...' Cyrus did not finish his explanation. He didn't need to.

'Cyrus, you idiot,' Joseph hissed the words for he did not want anyone else to hear them. 'You know what this makes you? It makes you a dealer. A drug dealer. The cops catch you peddling heroin, they'll give you ten, twenty years. No mercy, man.'

'Cocaine,' said Cyrus quickly. 'Cocaine, not heroin.' He said it as if it made a big difference to him, but it made none to Joseph.

'You are still a drug dealer.'

'I know, I know, but I was going to be on the streets. You know me, Joseph. You think I'd do something like this unless I really had to? I have to send money back home. I've got family relying on me. That money kept me in my room. It got the heating turned back on. You think I wanted to spend the winter sleeping in my cab. How would I survive that? Tell me!'

Joseph took another sip of his tea, to stop himself saying something he might regret. He was thinking how amazing it was that some things never changed. Cyrus and trouble had always gone hand in hand. If all the kids stole ice creams, only Cyrus would be caught with the evidence smeared across his face; if the whole class fooled around in school, it was Cyrus and Cyrus alone who ended up getting the cane. He was always too guileless, too much the underdog to get away with anything. Perhaps that was why Joseph always felt so obliged to look out for him.

When they were older, it was Joseph who became the rookie cop and Cyrus who had drifted from job to job. One night, Joseph learned about a police raid from his sergeant.

'Tonight we are taking down a bunch of snot noses who've been stealing cars and stripping them for parts. We are told they have an insider at old man Dehler's garage breaking them up after hours,' announced Sergeant Okuma. Then he smiled grimly, 'I've been told they will be resisting arrest and we are to teach them a lesson.'

Joseph was getting used to the excesses of some of his colleagues; beatings were a common method of controlling young criminals before they got too big. He also knew that the fledgling gang's biggest mistake had been failing to pay off the cops or pay tribute to the local crime boss, and that had sealed their fate. They had barely started before the bust was called in. Joseph wouldn't have cared if he had not recognised the name on Sergeant Okuma's lips, for he knew the mechanic who had been working all those late shifts down at Dehlers. It was Cyrus.

That night, Joseph drove his father's car down to the garage to intercept Cyrus before he went in. He knew that if he was seen with his friend, his police career would be over before it had started.

'But I have to go in, Joseph, the guys are expecting me. They have two more cars for me to work on.'

'And where do you think these cars came from, Cyrus?'

'Who knows? I don't, but I did not take them. Maybe they buy them.' His smile was broad. 'I'm just trying to make a little extra money here. Where's the harm in that?'

Joseph took a deep breath. 'The harm comes when the local crime boss gets upset by your friends' business venture and pays my superiors to close it down. Since they want to send out a warning to others, they are planning to break some arms and legs, maybe even some skulls.' Cyrus's smile vanished. 'I am here to prevent one of those skulls from being yours.'

'But if I'm not there, the guys will think...'

'Yes, they will, which is why you've got to leave Lagos tonight. It's your only chance,

Cyrus. Stay here and you'll get a beating from the cops, or your new friends will think you sold them down the river and they'll come after you.'

So Cyrus had gone, that same night, and his nomadic, unsettled existence had begun. Since that night, contact with Joseph had been just about the only constant in his ill-starred life.

It seemed Cyrus had learned nothing from his previous experience of crime however. Eventually Joseph looked up from his tea and asked, 'Why did you not come to me before, for help, before you did this crazy thing?'

'I couldn't come to you, Joseph. You've got the same problems as me, man. Worse, you've got a son to take care of. I couldn't burden you with this.'

But you'll burden me with it now, Joseph almost countered, when you might already be beyond my help. Instead, he allowed Cyrus to continue.

'After a few days, I told the man I'd made a mistake. I wasn't right for this kind of work and I had to stop.'

'And what did he say?' Once again, Joseph could have guessed. Cyrus looked truly scared at the memory.

'He told me it doesn't work like that. Once you start this thing, you don't stop until he tells you. I told him he could go to hell,

Joseph, but he threatened to kill me and I think he meant it.' There was disbelief in Cyrus's voice. He sounded like a child caught up in a dangerous, adult game, whose rules he could not possibly understand.

'Who is this guy?'

'His name is Ray.'

'Just Ray? That it?' asked Joseph.

'Yeah, to me, he's just Ray. These guys don't carry business cards.' He sounded annoyed now. 'He's always at the Meteor Club in Claremont. I think he runs it. I have to go down there later for another drop-off. This Ray, he looks like the kind of man who would kill someone. Joseph, what am I going to do?'

'Oh, Cyrus.' Joseph's frustration came from knowing there was no easy way out of the mess his friend was in. 'What else can you do but go to the police?'

'Are you crazy? If I talk to the police, he'll kill me for sure. You might as well put a gun to my head right now.' Joseph wanted to tell Cyrus the police would protect him, but he knew that was far from guaranteed. Cyrus could just as easily end up face down in the Bronx River. 'And have you forgotten? I'm not like you. I'm an illegal.'

'Cyrus, you've been here three years, you got a social security card. You pay taxes. Half the low-pay workers in New York are illegal. Who else are they going to get to pull

38

their drinks, make their beds and drive their cabs? If they arrested everybody who was in the country without proper papers their whole economy would collapse.'

'I've got social security but no Green Card and I'm a Muslim. Sure they don't mind a few illegal Mexicans, as many as you like, but do you want to bet what the police will do to me – a Muslim and an illegal in America after 9/11? Fit me for one of those orange suits, blindfold me, then fly me off to Cuba that's what. They'll lock me up in Camp X-Ray then forget about me! This ain't really the land of the free, Joseph, that's all bullshit. It's just something they all sing about. You got to have money to be free in this country!'

The two men on the next table looked over at Cyrus and he immediately fell silent, as if he regretted the outburst. They went back to drinking their teas and he continued in a lower voice. 'I can't do it, but what can I do? I can't keep on with the deliveries, either, so I'm screwed whatever. That's why I came to you, Joseph. You're smart.' And Joseph could see the desperate look of hope in his friend's eyes. Cyrus looked up to Joseph as an educated man, a man with answers.

'Are you still planning on going down there later and fronting it out with this guy?'

'To tell you the truth,' said Cyrus. 'I don't know.'

Joseph exhaled. 'Want me to go with you? I can't do it now, but maybe tonight while Yomi's at baseball.'

'Would you do that for me?' asked Cyrus in genuine awe.

'You know I would, though it doesn't mean I'm happy with you right now. I'm just trying to make sure you don't say the wrong thing and get your head blown off.'

'Thank you, Joseph.' And there was no mistaking his gratitude. 'But you know it might be dangerous.'

'*Might* don't come into it,' said Joseph grimly.

3

'It's good, huh?'

'Mmm,' replied Yomi, shovelling another forkful of chow mein into his mouth. The Chinese food had congealed in its cartons and the cab was going to smell of it for days, but at least Yomi didn't seem to mind the warmed-up food. He and his father sat at an ancient rickety table, eating straight from the cartons. Joseph pretended it was because Yomi preferred it that way, but it was mainly so he didn't have to wash the dishes later.

Their apartment in the Highbridge projects was tiny and the area a lot rougher than Joseph would have liked to bring up an eleven-year-old boy in but he didn't have any other option. At least the rent was low rate, the apartment clean and rodent free, and he aimed to keep it that way.

Joseph had a bedroom and there was a box room just big enough for Yomi and his things. The bathroom had barely enough space for its shower, toilet and chipped washbasin, and it was always damp from the poor ventilation, so he was constantly wiping mildew from the tiles. The area they were sitting in served as living room, dining room and kitchen. There was an ancient gas oven against the far wall and a couple of cupboards, separated from the living area by a flimsy wood and Formica worktop.

Joseph finished his meal quickly so he could mend his son's ripped blazer. The pocket had been torn off, Yomi claimed, by a doorknob, but Joseph wasn't sure he could believe that. He squinted at the little stitches. They were so loose it looked like a blind man had tried to repair the damage. He'd have to unpick them and start again once his son had gone to bed. He couldn't have him going to school looking like his father didn't care.

'How was school?' he asked, hoping Yomi wouldn't notice the mess he was making.

'Okay,' Yomi answered in that guarded way all schoolchildren have.

'What are you learning about these days?'

'Oh, you know...'

'No,' answered Joseph. 'I don't know, or I wouldn't ask.'

'Native Americans, how they used to be in the Bronx, before the Europeans kicked them all out.'

'Oh,' said Joseph, noticing a surly tone from his son. 'And was it a Native American who ripped your blazer with his tomahawk?'

Yomi looked down at his food. 'I told you it was a doorknob.'

Just then there was a rap at the door. It was Eddie, breathless from the climb up the stairs. 'Bad time?' he asked.

'No, my friend, come in, we always have time for you.'

Eddie had to duck to get beneath the doorframe, and Joseph could well imagine what the retired police sergeant was like in his prime: a tough guy commanding respect from colleagues and criminals alike. These days, he was getting thin, and crossed the room slowly with a stoop. Eddie always said his joints were twenty years older than the rest of him. His eyesight was going, too, 'betraying me' as he quaintly put it. Joseph didn't know for sure, but he guessed the death of Eddie's wife, ten years before, had something to do with the downturn in his health. The pictures in Eddie's apartment showed a happy couple. That was before her cancer set in.

'Ain't staying long, I brung you the news.' He handed Joseph the *New York Times* and the *New Jersey Observer* which he still bought every day so he could read up on his old neighbourhood.

'Hi, Eddie,' said Yomi, his voice muffled by the last fork full of chow mein. 'Is that the *New Joisy Obsoiver?*' Eddie's pronunciation was one of their recurring jokes.

'It sure is, sport.' Eddie beamed back at the boy in the indulgent manner of a man whose own kids had grown up and left him long ago.

'Don't talk with your mouth full, Yomi.' Joseph gave his son a look that said, 'How many times have I got to tell you?' Yomi grinned sheepishly back at him. 'Go and get your baseball kit together so we can leave right after Eddie and I have had coffee.'

''Bye, Eddie,' said Yomi, dropping out of the chair and running off to his bedroom.

'Kids!' smiled Eddie. 'Run everywhere, don't they? Even though they got all the time in the world.'

Joseph made two mugs of instant coffee then ushered Eddie to his usual seat, before taking the only other armchair the room possessed. He always made sure his friend had the best, most comfortable chair. For

43

his part, Eddie pretended not to notice the patches on the arms and the holes in the carpet and the drapes.

Joseph knew they were an unlikely pair, the retired Irish-American cop, as much a part of New York as the Carnegie Deli, and the detective from Lagos reduced to driving a cab around all day long, but they were glad of each other's company. For Eddie there was a chance to talk about the job he did for forty years on the other side of the Hudson River to someone who understood. Joseph was good company now Eddie's daughters had both moved out of the city. Most evenings after Yomi had gone to bed, Eddie padded up the stairs to knock softly on Joseph's door for a nightcap, always Irish whisky with Eddie, never scotch. Joseph never really drank before he came to America, but now he could see no good reason not to. He didn't mind the late visits from Eddie, looked forwards to them in fact. It was not as if he slept much these days.

'So, what's up, Eddie?' asked Joseph as the other man slurped his coffee.

Eddie made a noise that sounded something like 'nyah', which was the usual beginning to one of his rants about the state of the city, the limitations of his police pension, or the idiocy of one George Bush Junior, but this time he simply said, 'It's my daughter, the eldest, getting a divorce.'

'Sorry to hear it.'

'Well don't be, guy's an ass-wipe. He ain't no loss, but I do worry about her. You remember their daughter. She don't take after her old man, thank Christ. I tell you, Joseph, that little girl, she is just about the best thing in my sorry life. Anything bad ever happen to my granddaughter I don't know what I'd do.' The big old police man clenched his fists to illustrate his point. 'I think he's gonna try and take the girl from her mom.'

Joseph frowned his concern. 'I thought they usually leave kids with their mother.'

'Usually they do, and there ain't no reason why that ought to change,' cautioned Eddie. 'But you never know with the courts, you just never know, so it's a strain.' He tapped his chest right where his heart was. 'You know what I mean.'

'I understand. You are a father like me. You never stop worrying about your children, no matter how old they get.' Particularly when they come home with a torn blazer and no good reason for it, he could have added.

'Ain't that the truth. Just when you think they are out of your hair, they go and have their own kids.'

'And the worrying starts all over again.'

'Ha, you got it, my friend.' Eddie pointed to a battered paperback between them. It was open and print-side-down on the tiny table. A pneumatic blonde on the cover was tugging at the arm of a handsome private-eye type, who was firing a gun at some anonymous villain off the page. Joseph picked these paperbacks up for next to nothing, and they were as good a cure for insomnia as anything. 'How you getting on with that one?'

'Not so good. Someone's killing bar owners and the cops are baffled.'

'You don't say,' replied Eddie. 'Seems to me the cops are always baffled in these stories.'

'Which reminds me. I've got another one for you.'

'Go on,' said Eddie, his eyes lighting up.

'Why is it, whenever a witness is in danger of being murdered by gangsters and the hero can't even trust his own colleagues in the police department to keep that witness safe, he always takes this most dangerous person to stay with his sister, girlfriend or daughter, and they end up dead or in a coma, too?' Joseph spread his palms in astonishment. 'Why would you do that?'

'My friend, you wouldn't, not unless you was dumber than shit. Talking of the cops,' added Eddie, and Joseph knew what was coming. 'I guess you ain't heard back yet.'

'I was going to tell you tonight. The letter was waiting for me when I walked in.'

'And?' asked Eddie.

'It's a "no".'

'Jesus Christ,' muttered Eddie bitterly. 'I don't believe it. The experience you got. I hear they're taking guys fresh from Iraq, just out of one uniform and already looking to wear another. Some of them are so fucked up on drugs, already got the thousand-yard stare and a trigger finger that's itchier than a skank-whore's underwear. They'll be offing civilians and each other before you know it, let alone the gangsters. These guys don't know what it means to pull a gun and put it away again without loosing off a magazine. And they turn you down, the experience you got. How can they?'

'They tell me there's a problem.' Joseph appreciated Eddie's support but he didn't really feel like talking about this right now, it was still too raw. 'At the Nigerian end.'

'Someone's fucking you over? Saying you're no good?'

'That's not it exactly. It's sketchy, but when I phoned to talk about it all I got from the guy on the line was an off-the-record hint that the absence of a kind word from home was holding things up. It seems that until they say I was a good little boy, the NYPD are reluctant to take me on but that does not necessarily prevent me from trying again another time, apparently.'

'So it could just be a hold-up? You think?'

'Maybe,' agreed Joseph, but that was not what he thought. This absence of a positive reference was not part of the deal he'd struck. It was amazing how easy it had been to get the right papers and even arrange a Green Card while he was still in the country, when everybody had agreed it would be better for Joseph and Yomi to leave Lagos. Joseph was told he had too many powerful enemies. According to Captain Opara, his safety could no longer be guaranteed. Surely he could see that now, after what had happened to his wife. Better he took his son away with him to start a new life in the United States. The Americans were always looking for good, incorruptible men like Joseph to join their fine police force. All the references would be provided so that he would simply walk into a job there.

Now it seemed all that had changed. Joseph had applied twice already and been turned down both times. Someone didn't want Joseph to progress. He decided to change the subject. 'You hear about that shooting four blocks from here? Someone blew a cab's window out, killed the passenger, driver got away.'

'Yeah, I heard that. Bad business.' Eddie prided himself on missing nothing that happened in his neighbourhood.

'Quite strange,' said Joseph.

48

'I don't know,' said Eddie. 'Over the river, a few years back, three cab drivers got popped one after the other.'

'Cyrus said something about that. Was it the same?' Joseph couldn't disguise his interest. 'Shot through the windshield?'

'Nah. The MO was different. The perp sat in the back of the cab like a normal fare, got the driver to park up some place quiet then does him in the back of the head with a .45. Caused quite a panic at the time, all the drivers started putting bulletproof glass in after that. FBI came down and took the case over but in the end they didn't get no-wheres. Ended up a cold case, unsolved, no one even worked out what it was all for. Killings stopped after a while though.'

'Any idea why?'

Eddie shrugged. 'Maybe someone killed the killer, or the shooter got busted on some other rap and went down? Who knows.' Eddie drained the last dregs of his coffee. 'Hey, maybe they'll find a witness to this one, some platinum blonde the mob is after. You can bring her home wit' ya.'

'If she is young and beautiful, I will let her stay with you.'

'Ha, it might almost be worth it. The mob can shoot me afterwards and I'll die a happy man.'

They drank their coffee in silence for a moment but Joseph could not let the shooting go. 'Who'd want to kill a cab driver?' he asked almost as if he was talking to himself.

'I wouldn't worry, Joseph, you ain't one of those kind of drivers.'

'What kind is that?'

'The kind that do jobs for gangsters, you know, drug pick-ups and drop-offs.'

'Really?' asked Joseph trying not to think about Cyrus and his gangster.

'We've seen a little of it over the years. Puerto Ricans used to operate that way to avoid police surveillance, though I hear they are being driven out these days.'

'Who by?' asked Joseph, intrigued now by Eddie's inside knowledge.

'Dominicans, the Afro-Caribbean gangs. I saw what they were like when I was out there.' He nodded towards the window. 'Even more ruthless than the other guys and that's all it takes, Joseph, a bit more muscle and a worse rep than the people you're driving out.

'A few years back, we launched this big operation against crack houses. They were in the projects, selling drugs from holes they drilled through the walls. You'd walk into one apartment, guy would push the score through to you from the next one. So one day we come down on 'em hard, took out a load of dealers in the same raid. I mean this was big. There was FBI, DEA, SWAT teams all over. It made the evening news.'

'But you didn't get everybody?'

'Not even close to the big guys,' admitted Eddie. He took a noisy slurp of his coffee then sighed. 'There's a whole ring of low-level dealers still doing time. Not one of them rolled over on the men at the top.'

'Loyalty or fear?'

'Ha, it weren't loyalty, Joseph, this ain't the Cosa Nostra. None of these guys likes doing ten years, but they figure it's better than a shorter sentence they ain't never going to finish. It doesn't stop once they're inside, the gangs just carry on like before, only difference is, in a prison, when your own crew wants you dead for being a rat, there ain't no place to run.'

Eddie leaned forwards in his chair and slapped a hand to the back of his neck, kneading a sore muscle there. 'The new gangs, they ain't nice people. They started out selling to kids outside schools, then a few years went by and they got big enough to go after the Hispanics' territory. They took over big parts but not all of it. This war ain't over yet, it's still going on out there, every night, but the way I hear it the Puerto Ricans are losing. I hear they're now the ones selling to the schools, a sure sign of desperation.'

'Schools? Round here?' Joseph's thoughts immediately turned to Yomi.

'Ain't one in this district where a kid can't

get a cheap score if they want one. They get 'em hooked young.' Joseph's face must have betrayed his feelings because Eddie added, 'But you got nothing to worry about. Yomi's a good kid.' Just then Yomi appeared, carrying his baseball mitt, a bag strung over his shoulder. 'Talk of the devil and he shall appear!' blurted out Eddie. 'Anyhow, that was all years ago and it ain't like that no more.' Joseph understood that he was trying to put him at ease. 'It was a bad time, I tell you, Yomi, back then, even the rats walked round here in pairs.'

Yomi laughed.

'Hit a Homer for me tonight, sport,' said Eddie and he reached out and gave Yomi a manly pat on the side. Yomi winced, even though the contact was minimal.

'Come here, Yomi,' said Joseph quietly and the boy walked reluctantly up to his father.

Joseph tugged the boy's shirt up. There was a vivid patch of purple bruising that spread all along his side and over his ribs.

'Jeez, Yomi,' said Eddie. 'You get hit by a truck?' Joseph gave Eddie a look. 'I better let you guys get on,' added the old man quickly, as he heaved against the corners of the armchair.

'We'll talk about this on the way,' Joseph told his son, who looked as if he would rather do anything but that.

'I'll see you later maybe, Joseph?' said

Eddie as he reached the door.

'I hope so, I got the bottle in.' He nodded at the sideboard. They took it in turns to provide the whisky and it was Joseph's this time. Eddie glanced at the label and nodded approvingly. 'Bushmills? Good man.'

Joseph was far from a connoisseur of the 'water of life' as Eddie called it, but he enjoyed the ritual of their nightcap just as much as his friend. 'That's what it means in Gaelic, Joseph,' Eddie explained to him the first night they drank together. 'Literally, the water of life. What a fine way to describe something eh?'

Joseph didn't know too much about that but he understood the gentle way the whisky had of dulling his senses, preventing him from lying awake all night thinking about Apara. He'd always loved her name, it was as beautiful as she was and turned out to be entirely fitting. Translated it meant 'she who comes and goes'.

Yomi grabbed one of the little brown bags from the table and Joseph asked, 'What are you doing?'

'Bringing the fortune cookies,' explained his son. Yomi loved to break open the fortune cookies. He always pulled out each message with such reverence, like it was a treasure map or a coded signal only he could understand. Joseph wasn't big on fortune cookies. He didn't believe in that sort of thing. He knew nobody could predict their future. In this life you never could tell when something really bad was just around the corner. The hit man who decided to go out in his shiny, white Mercedes that day had no sixth sense it was going to be his last drive. He hadn't realised Joseph was closing in and certainly had no way of knowing that the men who hired him were going to make damn sure he never talked to anyone from the NPF, least of all Inspector Joseph Soyinka, a marked man, a cursed man from that day on.

4

They drove in silence for a time, Yomi staring fixedly out through the passenger window, avoiding his father's eyes. Joseph left him alone, hoping his son might eventually offer an explanation for his injuries but, once it became clear he had nothing to say, his father sighed. 'Are you going to tell me how you got those bruises or were you attacked by another doorknob?'

'You wouldn't understand.' Yomi's voice was distant, resentful and Joseph realised this was the first time his son had ever spoken to him like he was an outsider.

'Wouldn't I?'

'No.'

Joseph tried to adopt a kindly tone. 'Is that because I'm stupid or just so old I couldn't possibly remember what it is like to be your age?' Yomi did not respond.

'Or both maybe?'

Still there was no reply and Joseph was losing patience; his anger bubbling to the surface. If he had ignored his father like this back in Lagos when he was a child, he'd have felt the sharp crack of his hand; which was a step up from the leather belt his grandfather used on his father. Joseph would never dream of hitting Yomi, but he was damned if he was going to be taken for a soft touch because of it. He took a sudden left turn and the cab shot off the Expressway so sharply it made Yomi start as they veered away into a darkened side street.

Joseph was familiar with the road and knew it would be deserted. There was just a smattering of shabby buildings, in between the vacant lots, that housed small businesses somehow surviving against the odds, despite competition from the K-Marts, Wal-Marts and shopping malls that undercut them so effortlessly. There was an ethnic butcher's, a gun shop with metal shutters across its windows, a tattooists, and a pawn brokers with a jagged crown of razor wire along its roof. Even the lowlifes had no cause to come down here at night. Joseph pulled the car up abruptly by the side of the road. Yomi flushed, as if he suddenly grasped the seriousness of his father's mood.

'You are going to tell me what happened, Yomi, or I'll turn the cab round right now and you can forget about baseball.'

Yomi looked down at his shoes and muttered something inaudible.

'What?'

'I got into a fight.'

'That much I worked out for myself. Who were you fighting and why?'

'It was nothing. It doesn't matter.' His son looked on the verge of tears by now. It was costing him this much just to concede the bare fact of the fight to his father.

'Well it must have been something.'

'It wasn't anything, can't you just leave it? Why does there have to be a reason?'

With a heavy heart Joseph realised his son might have a point. In the South Bronx there didn't always need to be a reason for someone to take a beating.

'So you don't want to talk to me about it?'

'No!' said Yomi, as if his father had finally realised something that should have been obvious from the beginning. For the thousandth time Joseph questioned if he had the faintest idea how to be a good parent without Apara's loving guidance. The energy for

56

the quarrel left him.

'Okay, I'll let it drop, this time, and I'll take you to baseball practice but this better be the last I hear about you fighting. I didn't bring you to America so you could get into trouble and waste your life. Imagine what...' he stopped suddenly for he was about to say 'imagine what your mother would think' and he wasn't about to make the poor boy feel that bad '...Eddie would think,' he concluded hastily.

'He'd understand,' said Yomi sharply. The tears he'd been fighting finally started to flow.

Maybe he would, thought Joseph, as he realised how wretched his boy must have felt, sniffing back tears in the darkness by some derelict store, in a land that was still so foreign to them both. Perhaps Eddie would understand what Joseph seemed incapable of accepting, that sometimes boys fight no matter what you do. It's in their nature.

Joseph took a small packet of tissues from his jacket pocket and handed them to his son.

'Dry your eyes before we collect Freddie,' he said gently and the boy took the tissues.

Joseph realised with some helplessness that, as he was lecturing Yomi, he had begun to use phrases his own father had used on him. He turned the car around and rejoined the Expressway.

Joseph reached the shabby front door of the Impala, already opened a crack in invitation. The sound of deep African voices raised in animated conversation drifted out to greet him upon a wave of loud music. He dragged the heavy door open and a crisp flake of red paint peeled away in his hand, leaving yet another patch of bare wood. Were they ever going to give this old place a lick of paint?

The place was packed, but he instantly made out the tall, gangling figure perched precariously on a stool by the counter top. For some reason Cyrus had a broad smile upon his face.

'Joseph, it's okay,' said Cyrus as Joseph reached him, and he handed his friend one of those old-fashioned, glass bottles of Coca Cola that are shaped like an hour glass. 'Everything is going to be alright.'

That sounded unlikely. 'What?' asked Joseph.

'After you left, I got to thinking. It's so good of Joseph to come with me. He understands men like these better than I do. He has dealt with them before.'

'The slight difference being I used to have a badge and sometimes a gun,' said Joseph.

'Exactly,' agreed his friend. 'That's what I realised. Here is Joseph, I told myself, he is no longer a big shot detective, he has a young son and I'm asking him to go into this dangerous place with me at night, it's not right.' Cyrus shook his head. 'I couldn't expect you to do it.' He took a long swig from his bottle of Coke. 'So I went there myself this afternoon and talked to Ray.'

'You did?' asked Joseph in disbelief. 'What happened?' He could see his friend had obviously survived the confrontation but he wasn't sure how.

'I told him it all again, how I'd made a mistake and I was very sorry for his troubles but I couldn't carry on working for him no more.'

'And he was happy to hear this?'

'I expected he would not be. I think he will threaten me again, so I will have to reason with him, but you know what happened?' asked Cyrus rhetorically. 'He tells me it's cool.'

Joseph frowned. 'He said that?'

'Those exact words.' Cyrus spread his palms. '"It's cool." He says he doesn't want people working for him who don't want to do it because it's too dangerous for him. He tells me to keep quiet and not go to the police and I just laughed. No way I'm going to the police I tell him and once again he says "then it's cool."' And his smile was a hundred-watt bulb. 'Let's me walk right out of there.'

'Well, I wasn't expecting that,' conceded

Joseph. 'But why the sudden change of heart?'

'I don't know and to tell you the truth I don't need to know. Maybe his old lady been treating him good that day, maybe I just ain't worth the trouble of killing, we'll never know,' said Cyrus smiling, 'but I can't tell you how happy I am. It's like I've been given a second chance and I'm never going to mess up again. This I promise you now.'

'You'd better not.'

Just then the music in the bar stopped abruptly and everyone in the room suddenly fell silent. 'What's happening?' asked Cyrus.

Joseph had his back to the door so he did not see them walk into the Impala but when he turned around he could tell who they were instantly. Even in plain clothes, cops still looked like cops the world over – whether you were in Lagos or New York. Then he noticed the blue light blinking through a tiny crack in the shuttered windows and realised they had squad cars parked outside. The uniformed guys would stop anyone else from entering while the plainclothes men filed into the room before anyone could leave. In no time they'd identified and blocked all the exits. Stocky plainclothes officers in sports jackets and leather coats stood by every door and against each window with their arms folded. No one was going anywhere.

There was a woman in charge, a world-weary, stern-looking, forty-something redhead with a tough, no-nonsense demeanour. The stresses of her job were there for all to see in the lines on her face. She stood at the top of the steps by the door where she could overlook them and be seen by everyone. She took the silence, which instantly descended, as her right and wasted no time addressing them. While she spoke, the handful of, mostly white, men that fanned out either side of her scanned the room suspiciously.

'NYPD! Listen up!' she called hoarsely. 'Nobody leaves the building until we say so.' When he realised there was no way out of the Impala, a look of sheer panic crossed Cyrus's face. The next comment could have been addressed to him alone. 'We know some of you are here illegally but that doesn't concern us right now. This is a murder enquiry.'

'You see,' whispered Joseph.

'She's a cop,' answered Cyrus. 'They lie to everyone.'

The officer continued self-importantly, 'My name is Assistant Chief McCavity of the 41st precinct. All we want to do is talk to you about this afternoon. A young woman has been murdered, gunned down in cold blood, in a taxi cab, in broad daylight, right in the middle of the street.'

There was not an ounce of subtlety about this investigation, thought Joseph. McCavity had just given everything away. She'd told the entire room who she was and what she wanted, surrendering any advantage surprise might bring her. Joseph was astounded she had shown her hand so early. Surely there was nothing to be gained from it, except maybe the intoxicating feeling of power over a room full of scared strangers.

'We are acting on information received and I ask you all to remain seated while my officers move among you with some questions. Nobody leaves till then but, if you assist us, this shouldn't take too long.' She concluded with little apparent conviction, 'The New York Police Department thanks you for your cooperation at this time.' She could have been reading the words from a diversity card provided by the Human Resources department.

As soon as McCavity was through, the room became filled with the buzz of a dozen animated conversations. Her officers began to move among the tables in ones and twos clutching pictures of the dead girl, notebooks at the ready. Joseph watched them as they worked their way towards the rear of the Impala, where Cyrus sat wringing his hands. His friend clearly did not trust McCavity's calming words about his illegal status. He looked terrified.

It didn't take long before one of the officers picked up a stool and dragged it towards them. He was a big man in his early thirties with close-cropped dark hair and stubble across his chin. He wore a long, black leather jacket that made him look more like a nightclub doorman than a police detective.

'How you doin'? I'm Detective Baker,' he said as he sat down and took out a notebook and, before they could answer, he pushed an eight by ten photograph of a young girl under their noses and let it rest on the counter in front of them. 'This is Tina Ferreira, an office worker originally from Cuba. She's twenty one.' The officer paused to ensure he had their full attention. 'Or I should say she *was* twenty one. This afternoon she was killed when a bullet hit her in the head as she was travelling in a cab just a couple of blocks from here. We believe she is the innocent victim of a murder attempt on a driver who works this patch.'

Joseph scrutinised the photograph carefully. It showed a young, curly-haired Latino girl still in her teens, dressed in a stripy sweater, smiling at the camera. The picture looked a couple of years old, and was probably taken for a high-school yearbook or family get-together.

'Poor girl,' said Joseph. Tina looked so young and innocent in the picture. It was hard to imagine her cold body lying in the city morgue with her brains blown out.

'Yeah, the driver told us a guy jumped right out in front of his vehicle, pointed a gun straight at him, so he swerves see, but the bullet hits the poor young girl instead and it's goodbye, Tina.'

'That's real bad luck,' said Cyrus, 'but why you asking about it in here?'

'We're told a lot of cab drivers hang out in this joint.'

Anticipating his next question Joseph admitted, 'we're both drivers.'

Baker nodded as if he had just proved his point. 'Well, there you go. Either of you guys been approached by any gangs lately, asking for favours?'

'What kind of favours?' asked Joseph.

'Driving jobs, pick-ups, deliveries, you know. Little packages.' Then he suggested reasonably, 'you might not know what's in 'em.'

'No,' said Joseph.

'Me, neither,' added Cyrus a little too quickly.

Baker transferred his gaze from Joseph to Cyrus before continuing, 'Tell me, were either of you guys working round here when those cab drivers got whacked three years back. There were three of them in all.'

'I've only been here a year,' said Joseph.

'I heard something about that when I first

arrive,' said Cyrus, 'the others told me all about it. Terrible thing. Terrible.'

'And have either of you heard anything about this latest shooting? You know of any reason why anybody would want to shoot a cab driver?' Joseph almost told him there could be plenty of reasons. After all someone had pulled a gun on him that very morning, but he had no wish for the police to know about that. When they both told Baker they knew nothing about the killing he seemed to suddenly lose interest. 'If you hear anything about this one, you make sure you give us a call, yeah?'

'Of course, officer,' said Cyrus, nodding fiercely.

'Now if I could just see some ID and take a few personal details,' he added, raising his pen in readiness.

At every table they went through the same routine. Everyone was shown the same photograph of Tina Ferreira's smiling, pretty young face then asked if they knew anything about the cab killings. Detective Baker had moved to another table and Joseph and Cyrus were left to wait till all the interrogations were complete. They sat in a respectful silence that enabled Joseph to pick up threads of other conversations. It was mostly inconsequential stuff, no one seemed to know anything but just as the police were wrapping up their enquiry, Joseph overheard a young detective asking one of the older drivers what he knew about the shooting. Most of the conversation was indistinguishable above the noise in the room but the old guy's reply to one question caught Joseph's attention. 'If you ask me, it was her job that killed her,' he said, and there was something in the way he spoke that made Joseph assume he knew the victim, at least in passing, but what could he mean by that crack about her job? The NYPD said the girl was hit by a stray bullet meant for somebody else, so what did her line of work have to do with it?

Joseph leaned forwards and whispered to Cyrus, 'Who's the old guy talking to the young detective in the suit?'

Cyrus whispered back, 'That's Samuel, been driving a cab round here since Madonna was a virgin.'

Before he could think on this any further, there was a commotion of scraped chairs and excitable conversation and Joseph noticed people were starting to leave. He now realised what McCavity's plan had been all along. She allowed those who could prove who they were and where they worked to go – everybody except the cab drivers, around a dozen of whom were left spread out glumly between half-empty tables.

McCavity rose once more. 'Thank you for

your continued patience. There is one last thing we need from you. We are going to take a look at all of your cabs and before anybody starts quoting the law, we don't need a warrant – they are all classified as public vehicles, so please just cooperate.'

Cyrus whispered to Joseph, 'What am I gonna do? They'll find traces of blow in the glove compartment.'

'Calm down, Cyrus, they don't have sniffer dogs and they're not looking for anything like that today.'

But Cyrus's panic was rising. 'You realise how close I was to that shooting today?' He grasped his friend's forearm tightly.

'No, because you didn't tell me,' answered Joseph through gritted teeth. 'And you are starting to act like a suspect.'

Cyrus let go of his arm. 'You are right, Joseph.' He took a deep breath. 'I have nothing to hide.' He seemed to be saying it as much to convince himself as his friend. 'I just don't like the police.' He gave a half-hearted smile. 'No offence.'

'None taken,' said Joseph wearily.

The entire party was taken down to the cab firm. The garage was an underground sub-let beneath an office block that smelt overpoweringly of damp and engine oil. The drivers were lined up against a stained, white wall bathed by the inadequate brightness from an elderly striplight that cast dark shadows whenever anyone moved. Each man was asked, in turn, to identify then open up his cab, before stepping back while the officers went to work on it. After a time, it began to look as if this might be a fruitless exercise and the drivers started to lose their collective sense of anxiety. Instead, it was gradually replaced by a kind of frustrated boredom.

Joseph had already admitted his cab was parked in a nearby side street and consented to have it searched later for, unlike Cyrus, he really did have nothing to hide. Cyrus's cab was the fourth to be searched and he stood silently while Detective Baker, wearing rubber gloves, felt around under the dash then beneath the seats.

'Holy shit,' he said as his rear end backed out of the car. 'Look what I got.' And when his head came up he was smiling, for in his gloved hand was a .45 calibre automatic pistol, its trigger guard speared by the pencil he was holding.

5

The moments just before Cyrus was arrested for the murder of the young girl came back to Joseph as a blur. He recalled how two detectives had grabbed Cyrus, who began to protest. Then, when his panic rose, Cyrus started jabbering and swearing at them and flailing his arms, so they threw him facedown across the bonnet of his cab, cuffed his hands behind his back and led him away. Joseph would never be able to remember making a move towards them but he must have tried, for burly hands restrained him and authoritative voices urged him to calm down before he got himself into deep trouble.

Amidst the confusion, as Cyrus was led away, McCavity and her entourage walked right by Joseph, who struggled to break free. 'What are you doing?' he shouted, panic in his voice, and she stopped and turned to face him.

'I'm arresting this man for the murder of Tina Ferreira.'

'What? That's ridiculous, Cyrus is no murderer.'

'What are you? His mother?' asked Baker.

'No, I'm his friend and you are making a big mistake.'

'Really?' Baker seemed to bristle at the suggestion. 'You don't say? It's just that usually the friends and family of defendants are so quick to tell us "yeah you got the right guy he did it, put him away for life". In fact you could be the first who tried to convince us we got the wrong man.'

Joseph ignored the sarcasm. 'But he didn't do it.'

Baker was about to challenge him once more but McCavity stepped in. 'That's okay, Baker. What makes you so sure?' she asked Joseph, appearing to be genuinely interested in his point of view.

'You said you were acting on information received. I'd say you were given Cyrus as a fall guy.'

McCavity's tone was condescending. 'The information we received suggested a cab driver was involved. Then we found the gun in your friend's cab.'

'Conveniently,' said Joseph.

Again Baker leapt in, 'What do you mean?'

Joseph kept his voice deliberately calm, 'I watched you search the cabs, Detective Baker. You did the first three real quick like you weren't really expecting to find anything. When you took Cyrus's cab, instead of opening the trunk or the glove compartment you rummaged under the dash for a second then went straight beneath the seat and, big surprise, you found a gun.'

McCavity gave Baker a critical look that seemed to indicate her displeasure at his acting skills. Joseph continued, 'Straight-away you arrest Cyrus on suspicion of murder. Why? Because he had a gun in his cab. But it could have been any gun. You haven't had time to get ballistics reports and a .45 automatic has got to be a pretty common weapon for New York. Cyrus can't be the first cab driver you found carrying a little extra life insurance, that's assuming the gun is his and I'm here to tell you it's not. Cyrus is way too nervous to have an automatic in his cab. He'd be worried about blowing his own toes off.'

McCavity held her gaze on Joseph for a long while, then finally she said, 'So it wouldn't surprise you to learn we expected to find a gun in your friend's cab?'

'No, from the evidence of my own eyes it was obvious. You knew the gun was there all along. I'm telling you someone planted it and served you up a fall guy. The only question is why you would believe them.'

Another detective patted Joseph down and handed McCavity his wallet. Her eyes narrowed as she checked his identification then contemplated Joseph. 'Because we got a witness, Mr Solinka.'

'Soyinka.' Joseph corrected her.

71

She glanced down again at the name on his ID card. 'Yeah, that'll be it,' she said, as if Joseph had just offered up the correct answer to a crossword clue. 'Baker, I think Mr Soyinka had better come with us.' She jerked her head in the direction of the squad cars parked outside, and Joseph was bundled towards them.

'Are you arresting me? What for?'

'No, you are free to go if you wish.' She walked briskly, keeping up with her men as they steered Joseph towards the exit. 'But I thought you might want to help us exonerate your friend by joining a little ID parade.'

'Okay,' said Joseph. 'If that's what it will take.'

'You obviously think it won't be a problem but, like I say, we got a witness, Mr Soyinka, as well as the murder weapon and if the ballistics come back positive, which I think they will, and your friend Cyrus gets ID'd tonight then he is in a whole heap of shit, no matter what you say.'

McCavity turned back to Baker. 'We'll need another half-dozen drivers to volunteer for the line-up, Baker. Make sure they at least partially resemble the suspect for once.' Then she walked away, oblivious to the younger man's irritation at being left behind.

As Joseph was marched passed him, Baker

must have assumed McCavity was out of earshot for he muttered to a colleague, 'Should be easy enough, these spooks always look exactly the same to me.'

McCavity stopped in her tracks and turned to stare back at her officer. 'You keep talking like that, Baker, and I'll suspend you right here and now.'

'Oh, hey, I was only...'

'Shut up!' she barked, her voice echoing round the tight confines of the garage, and he immediately fell silent, as did everybody else. 'I don't have time for any of your racist shit right now. You want to make cracks like that, you don't do it on my watch. Do it here, in my precinct, and I'm the one who ends up on the front page of the *New York Times*, defending the force against an endemic culture of racism, not you. Fuck up again and the next time you come face to face with a member of the New York public you'll be asking them "do you want fries with that?"'

'Okay, okay,' Baker mumbled, sounding like a naughty schoolboy who is forced to apologise to the teacher in front of all his friends.

No one else said a word.

'Shape up,' she warned him and with that she was gone, the entourage trailing after her once more with Joseph in tow. He realised what a tight reign she kept on these macho men and he didn't suppose they liked it for one minute, but it was probably the only way a woman could stay in control here. Clearly McCavity was a formidable police officer but Joseph would have to try and find a way to deal with her or Cyrus was in big trouble.

The 41st precinct had been passed over when the refurbishment budgets were handed out. The interior walls of the old police building were almost entirely bare, except for a thin coat of yellow emulsion and some light-brown indents where chunks of plaster were missing. A couple of public-information notices were pinned lopsidedly onto a cork notice board halfway along to break the monotony.

The men chosen for the ID parade were kept waiting at the end of a long corridor. Joseph sensed their displeasure at missing valuable fares was tempered by relief they were not undergoing the same ordeal as Cyrus. Like Cyrus, most of these men shared a deep distrust of the police, so they would not have given much for their fellow driver's chances right now.

Joseph was permitted to make a phone call and he used it to arrange for Freddie's parents to explain to Yomi that he would be delayed. They would drop his son back at the project. Joseph was just glad he had trusted the boy with a key. He cited an emergency but did not explain its true nature to the other boy's parents. Yomi had enough trouble to contend with without the whole school knowing his old man was caught up in a murder enquiry. The parents seemed happy enough to help out, grateful for the toing and froing Joseph had done on their son's behalf in the past.

Joseph hurried back to the bright-orange, plastic chair he had been assigned, where a solitary cup of lukewarm coffee from the vending machine was thrust into his hand by a uniformed female police officer. The powdered drink they all received seemed to differentiate their status as reluctant helpers of police enquiries to that of common prisoners. Joseph needn't have rushed back. He hated sitting around like this, inactive and helpless, as events that were beyond his control unfolded around him. He remembered how Captain Opara made him wait outside his office before giving him the special assignment.

'You will receive the full backing of senior officers in the NPF and beyond. Important men from the government eagerly await the outcome of your investigation.'

Opara kept him waiting there a second time, when Oba Matusa had been found shot up next to his Mercedes. It was then Joseph found that the important men from the government and the senior officers he had heard so much about were no longer quite so firmly behind him. Though, through Captain Opara, they naturally expressed profound sadness for the loss of his wife and all of them apparently wished Inspector Soyinka well.

The drivers waited for more than an hour for the ID parade to commence, while a nearly spent lightbulb drove them all crazy as it blinked on and off above them. Joseph let his cup of powdered coffee go cold at his feet.

When Joseph finally walked out into the line-up he could not quite quell his feelings of apprehension. Though his prime concern was for Cyrus, he did not want to be picked out in error by a confused witness. After all, he had been at the scene of the crime, albeit moments after the action had taken place, and he didn't want to have to explain that to the police. The way this case was shaping up, the NYPD might be happy to settle for anyone, as long as they sent somebody down for a very long time.

The drivers all lined up as instructed and stared straight ahead. Before too long, a distraught-looking Cyrus was escorted into the room. He looked like a man being led to his execution.

'No talking,' a uniformed, male officer

warned them all.

Joseph was made to shuffle along so his friend could appear in the centre of the line-up. Cyrus did not dare to look directly at Joseph, let alone attempt to communicate with any of his fellow drivers. They, in turn, wanted to get the task over and done with as quickly as possible, so they could get back out on the streets and start earning again. The silence in the room was oppressive.

Finally Joseph became aware of the merest hint of a shadow behind the two-way mirror in front of them, or perhaps it was merely his imagination. Presently, a detective's deep, unemotional voice came over the intercom and asked number four to step forwards, then turn to the right, then back to the front and finally to return to the line-up.

Number four was Cyrus.

Suddenly, as abruptly as it had begun, the parade was at an end. Cyrus was man-handled away again, with no clue as to his perceived guilt or innocence in the eyes of the witness, but it did not look good to Joseph. The other drivers left the building as soon as they were excused but he remained behind, desperate for news of his friend. Joseph asked the officer on the front desk about Cyrus and was told that information was not available 'at this time'. Joseph wanted to ask when it would become available but the flat, humourless monotone of the officer warned him against it.

Just then, McCavity emerged and walked quickly by, flanked by two of her detectives. Joseph was surprised to see McCavity's hair had been brushed and styled and she was now wearing more make-up. He wasn't sure how to address her, but settled on "Miss McCavity". He called it loud enough for her to hear but she didn't pause for an instant and was out of the building before Joseph could think of anything else to add. The officer on the desk had turned his back on him now and he was still no nearer knowing whether Cyrus would be released or charged. Then Joseph noticed a short, harassed-looking young man emerging from the same corridor as McCavity. He was dressed in a creased suit, with a plain, white shirt and a crumpled tie. He carried a battered, leather briefcase in one hand and a small stack of cumbersome manila files in the other. This had to be the lawyer.

'Excuse me, sir,' said Joseph in his most formal English and the young man stopped in his tracks, taken aback at being afforded such a courtesy in the 41st precinct. At this stage in his short career he must be taking shit from all sides, thought Joseph, from the cops, the judges and most of his own clients. 'Are you representing Cyrus Agyeman?'

'Er ... yes, I am,' the man replied doubtfully, unsure what use Joseph would put this information to. 'But how could you know that?'

Joseph ignored the question and instead proffered his hand to the lawyer. 'I am his good friend Joseph Soyinka.'

The young man wedged the folders under his arm and took Joseph's hand. 'Henry Augsberger, public defender,' he said stiffly.

'I must talk to you about his case,' said Joseph, hoping the lawyer would assume he had important information to impart when it was actually the other way around. 'Let me help you with those.' And before the lawyer could protest, Joseph had relieved him off his load and was steering the younger man to another clump of plastic chairs in a quiet alcove, with a firm but gentle hand in the small of his back.

'Cyrus mentioned you, Mr....'

'Soyinka.' Surely it wasn't such a hard name to remember, but everybody in America seemed to forget it as soon as they heard it.

The lawyer nodded. 'He said "find Joseph, he will tell you everything", and here we are, I appear to have found you already.' He gave a nervous little laugh and Joseph wondered how many years he'd been out of college before they handed him this pro-bono murder case that nobody else wanted. 'So, go on.'

'By "everything" Cyrus simply means the truth, that he is not a murderer.'

'Mmm,' the lawyer nodded slowly, not bothering to hide his disappointment. 'Though he is, in point of fact, a drug dealer ... apparently.'

Joseph's heart sank as he wondered just how much Cyrus had admitted during that short interview, with his lawyer in the room to ensure he did not say anything that might incriminate himself. He contemplated arguing the difference between a drug dealer and a courier of drugs but decided against antagonising the young lawyer with semantics. 'Cyrus has recently become mixed up with some bad people, but he is no hit man. You have met him, right?'

'Of course, and he seems quite innocuous but then so do many criminals, Mr Soyinka, which is perhaps why many of them remain at large for so long. Cyrus doesn't look like a hit man but then who does? Now, I will be representing your friend to the very best of my abilities but, let's not bullshit one another here shall we? His chances are not great.'

'You mean they really are going to charge him with this girl's murder?'

The lawyer held out a hand and counted off the damning factors on his fingers one after the other. 'Well, let's see, shall we? He has no alibi, they have a gun, which they are confident will be a match for the murder weapon and they found this under the seat of your friend's vehicle. What's more, they have a witness who, without a moment's hesitation, just picked him out of an ID parade. Then we have the unfortunate occurrence of Cyrus having recently used his cab service as a front for dealing drugs. So, yes, in my considered professional opinion, they are likely to charge him.'

'With no motive and no connection to the victim, it looks like a classic set-up to me.'

'Really? Well forgive me if I don't offer that hypothesis to the jury. They are liable to be less than sympathetic to the notion of the NYPD setting up your friend.'

Joseph began to realise that, if you did not actually know Cyrus, his innocence might not be as plainly obvious as it should have been to the police. The light above his head began to flicker on and off again. Were the NYPD strapping someone to an electric chair in some other part of the building?

'Have the police been able to establish any link between Cyrus and the other driver or the dead girl?' asked Joseph.

'No, not yet and I have made that point most forcibly indeed. However they are confident that something will be uncovered eventually; drugs, vice...'

'Vice?'

'Who knows? Sexual obsession, domestic

dispute, I could go on.' He shrugged. 'Take your pick. They are sure they will uncover something.' He frowned at Joseph. 'I did advise Mr Agyeman not to offer up a defence of being a drug dealer to avoid being charged as a murderer, but he was quite adamant. He seemed to think this somehow gave him an alibi though of course it doesn't. It merely provides the police with a possible motive. He also told me afterwards that it was your idea. "Joseph told me to go to the police, Joseph told me to tell them everything."' Joseph's heart sank. Cyrus had not been looking at a murder charge when Joseph had given him this advice. 'Trouble is they don't much like drug dealers in New York. In my experience, just about the only folk who elicit less sympathy from a jury here are paedophiles.' He thought for a moment. 'With the possible exception of defence lawyers from Boston.' Then he smiled grimly. 'Me, I'm from St Louis.' He rose and scooped up his files. 'If the ballistics are confirmed, Cyrus will be charged, Murder One, and that's life Mr Soyinka. Good evening to you.' He nodded courteously and left Joseph alone with his thoughts.

Joseph looked in on Yomi and was pleased to see the boy was fast asleep in his bed. He looked again and noticed his son was still wearing his baseball glove. He smiled and gently removed the glove without waking him. Joseph wished rest could find him so easily.

It was late, but that hadn't bothered Eddie. While Joseph checked on Yomi, the old man poured them both a nightcap. Joseph knew he would be unable to sleep without one. Eddie had put the late news bulletin on but turned the volume down low so they could talk. He seemed to sense his friend had troubles.

'Everything okay?' he asked.

'Nope,' conceded Joseph and he told Eddie everything. How he had met Cyrus at the Impala only to have the cops burst in and take his friend away, following the discovery of the gun in his cab. Eddie listened carefully while Joseph completed the story of the ID parade and the lawyer's grim analysis of Cyrus's chances. Joseph was almost done when he noticed something over Eddie's shoulder.

'What is it?' asked Eddie.

'Can you turn up the volume?'

Eddie reached for the remote control. 'Sure.'

Joseph had spotted footage of Assistant Chief McCavity as she emerged from the 41st precinct. He would have recognised her even if the news bulletin had not assisted by putting her rank and name up as a caption on the bottom of the screen. McCavity was immediately accosted by a microphone-wielding TV reporter but she didn't seem to mind. Joseph remembered that although the presence of the reporter appeared to be a complete surprise to her, she'd had her hair fixed and makeup applied just before she left the building that night.

By the time he'd turned up the volume, McCavity was in full flow. '...represents a significant breakthrough in our investigation into the tragic death of Tina Ferreira, a young woman who, like millions before her, came to America to start a new life. Instead she was cruelly gunned down on the streets of the South Bronx, an innocent victim of another thoughtless gun crime. This was a life tragically and prematurely ended by a ruthless killer who missed his intended target, a New York cab driver with a clean record, and instead took the life of a poor young woman. I can confirm that we already have a suspect in custody and neither my officers nor I shall rest until we bring her killer to justice.'

'Sure you will,' snorted Eddie. 'Tonight you'll sleep like a baby.'

'You know her?'

'I know the name and I know the type,' he replied dismissively. 'And to think they turned you down.'

McCavity went on to describe Tina

Ferreira as a young woman of excellent character who fled Cuba in search of a better future and had worked hard in America, taking a job as an office temp and Joseph was immediately reminded of the old driver's comment. 'She was determined to make a contribution to this new land she loved and now called home,' concluded McCavity, who acted as if she was genuinely moved by the young girl's death.

'Bet she baked a mean apple pie, never gave head and always went to church on Sundays,' snorted Eddie.

'What?' Joseph was taken aback by his friend's cynicism.

'Well, it bugs me. The news people always do this. You could be the meanest son-of-a-bitch on the planet, all you gotta do is get yourself shot and they turn you into a saint. Do it in a police uniform and you get to be a hero as well – even if you knew nothing about it. Joseph, I've been to enough police funerals and most of them were stand-up guys but some of them were corrupt, crooked or just plain mean, yet they all got the same fucking eulogy from the chief of police and the same salute from the guys with the rifles and the white kit gloves. It gets me pissed that all you got to do these days is die for everyone to forget what a fucker you were when you was alive.'

Joseph shifted a little in his seat. 'The day

you die, Eddie, I'll tell everybody you were a plain-speaking man who was never afraid to speak out when he saw injustice.'

'You mean a nasty-minded prick,' laughed Eddie.

'You got it.'

The reporter asked McCavity about a link between the killing of the tragic Tina and previous murders in the area. She gave him a teasing answer. 'I am afraid I can neither confirm nor deny recent media speculation linking the alleged murder weapon in this case to that used in another recent killing.'

'Meaning it was,' said Eddie.

'Where do the press get this stuff?' asked Joseph.

'Leaked.'

'Yes, but by whom?'

Eddie nodded at the screen. 'Her.'

'You think so?'

Eddie leaned forwards in his chair, animated now. 'I know so, Joseph. Her kind won't go out in front of the press unless they know every question they are gonna be asked beforehand, so they make sure the reporters ask the questions they want to answer. I'm not saying she picked up the phone herself. I'm saying information like that has a tendency to reach journalists one way or another. Now she gets to look sharp on the TV news because we all think she's caught a two-time hit man, which ain't good for your friend's prospects of a fair trial when you think about it.'

The reporter persisted with his line of questioning. 'And what of speculation linking this killing with the so-called Bronx River Murders three years ago. The perpetrator of those three killings, whose victims were incidentally all cab drivers, was never caught, but we understand you could be close to a significant breakthrough in that case.'

'Oh my god,' said Joseph, 'they are going to try and pin those murders on Cyrus, too. This just gets worse.'

'Was he even in the country back then?'

'Yeah, just,' Joseph had to admit. Someone had done their homework on Cyrus before they framed him.

McCavity gave another half-hearted denial that left nobody in any doubt she had managed to catch a serial killer, clearing up five murders in the process, even before Cyrus had been charged and brought to trial. God help him, thought Joseph.

She concluded, 'I would like to pay tribute to the courageous witness who has agreed to testify. This man, who I obviously cannot name, feels terrible that a poor young woman was murdered in the back of his cab by a stray bullet that was clearly intended for him. He is determined to bring this killer to justice.'

There was some deft editing in the studio and footage appeared of the witness being escorted from the police station earlier, with a brown leather jacket draped over his head to mask his identity.

'Nice jacket for a cab driver,' said Eddie.

'What?'

'That's a Belstaff, a leather biker's jacket at the top end of the market, and they ain't cheap.'

The news programme cut back to the studio, where a serious-faced female reporter discussed the latest speculation. A picture of a man's face appeared on a screen over her left shoulder. He seemed no stranger to violence. 'Two days ago the body of Eduardo Pinto, a twenty-eight-year-old career criminal with previous convictions for drug dealing, was found in a dumpster just yards from the Yankee stadium. He was in the country illegally and is believed to be the latest victim of a wave of drug-related gangland killings that has plagued the South Bronx lately. Sources close to the police confirm the existence of a turf war between rival gangs attempting to seize control of the lucrative narcotics trade.'

While she was speaking, the screen cut to a montage of pictures, which began with the taped-off dumpster and continued to show hooded drug dealers standing on anonymous sidewalks before they handed small packages through the windows of cars as they slowed. It concluded with images of used syringes that had been found in local cemeteries and playgrounds. The reporter rounded up the story, stating that one of the preferred methods of transporting the drugs was to cajole innocent cab drivers into ferrying dealers from place to place. This appeared to provide a motive for the attack on an uncooperative cab driver.

'That's the wonderful world we live in and it looks like they are gonna blame the whole thing on your poor friend Cyrus.'

'It's crazy, Eddie. You've met Cyrus. You know he's no killer.'

Eddie seemed reluctant to state such a thing with conviction. 'I know it if you tell it to me, my friend. Trouble is the jury don't know any such thing.'

'It's a set up,' said Joseph, 'and it stinks. I thought this sort of thing only happened in Nigeria. Not here, not in America.'

'What? Because we got democracy? That's just a word, Joseph. We got more than our fair share of crooked, evil and corrupt bastards over here, from the White House right down through City Hall and the police precincts to the street corners, clip joints and clubs. For every good man I ever met who was trying to do what's right there's another, maybe two or three, trying to do him down and make a dishonest buck in the process. This whole world stinks, Joseph. The quicker you learn that the easier it'll be.'

Joseph nodded sadly. 'I know you are right, Eddie, but what the hell am I going to do?'

'You keep trying.' Eddie sat up in his chair then and smiled. He put up his big, gnarled fists. 'Let me tell you the way I see it; life is like a prize fight. You're up against a mean, tough, old bare-knuckle fighting son-of-a-bitch, and he fights dirty. He'll kick you, gouge your eye and spit in your face, but if you keep hitting him, he's got to fall eventually.' He landed a couple of mock jabs close to Joseph's chin. 'You just keep hitting him now, you hear?'

After Eddie had gone, Joseph toyed with the idea of going to bed, but the events of the day kept racing through his mind. He sat down in his battered armchair, poured himself another measure of whisky and looked out through the window at the city lights down below. He let the liquid gently burn the back of his throat, then felt its soothing qualities as the alcohol hit the spot. Only this time it didn't make him feel much better. Cyrus was still facing a murder rap and it was at least partly Joseph's fault for giving him such damn-fool advice. What an idiot he had been.

Joseph knew his friend was no murderer, so someone was trying to pin a contract killing on an innocent man. But why Cyrus? It was not as if he had a long list of enemies. Until recently nobody ever had a bad word to say against him. Then came the meeting with the mysterious Ray, the extra shifts as a drug courier and the ill-advised attempt to quit the work against the wishes of his narcotics-dealing employer, who had strangely relented and set him free from his obligations a few hours before the police found a gun in Cyrus's cab. It was then and only then that Cyrus's life had begun to implode. For the sake of an extra few hundred dollars in dirty money, Cyrus was looking at thirty years in a state penitentiary. Thirty years, just thinking about it took your breath away. He'd be an old man by the time he was released. That's if he survived the experience, and Joseph could not see any way his friend was going to cope. He was too gentle, too easily beset by gloom, even in the outside world, to cope with years staring at a prison wall. Joseph sipped his whisky and wondered what the hell he was going to do to get Cyrus out of this unholy mess.

6

The next day, Yomi spotted one of his friends and was out of the car in a hurry. A quick "Bye dad", called over his shoulder as he ran off, was the only clue their relationship had been restored to some level of normality following the tension of the previous night. Their little domestic row seemed to be the least of Joseph's worries now. As usual he had begun his day feeling weary, the product of a troublesome night's sleep, the restlessness caused, as much as anything, by the thought of his close friend spending the night alone in a police cell. He knew Cyrus must be scared out of his wits.

Edging his cab away from the steps of the school, carefully avoiding the children that were milling all around, Joseph was about to head off when he spotted an attractive woman making her way across the parking lot. Her long, dark hair was tied back for the school day and, though her clothes were practical enough, they seemed somehow to cling to her body. Brigitte DeMoyne was one of those women who could look good in anything.

Brigitte was a bright, permanently cheerful, history teacher in her mid thirties. Joseph had first spoken with her on a parents' evening and discovered she had been a traveller, working in Africa in her twenties, even spending time in Lagos. Now he pulled up alongside her and wound down the window.

She greeted him with a broad smile. 'Joseph. Hi. Nice to see you.'

'Hello, Brigitte, you, too, have you got a moment, or is this a bad time?'

The teacher looked round at the kids as they streamed into the old school building from all angles.

'Sure,' she said and began to fidget with her handbag, transferring it from one hand to the other as they talked.

'It's just I'm a little worried about Yomi right now. He came home yesterday covered in bruises. He'd been in some sort of fight.'

'Oh dear.' Her smile vanished. 'That doesn't sound like our Yomi. He never gets into trouble – one of only a very few I could say that about. You want me to keep an eye out for him?'

'If you can, I mean I know how busy you are but...'

She held up a hand to him. 'I'll do what I can.'

'Thanks, I really appreciate that.' He nodded towards the building. 'How have things been here lately?'

'I'll be honest with you, Joseph, like a lot of schools in this district we've had our problems. The Principal secured funding for metal detectors and now we have to carry out random searches on the kids.'

'I got a letter about that. You didn't get any complaints from me at the time. Not if it stops them carrying knives.'

'Shame though, isn't it,' she said. 'Sign of the times, I guess.'

Then she started, as she realised all the kids had abruptly disappeared. 'I'm really sorry, I have to go or I'll be late for class and that wouldn't be good, as I'm the teacher.' She raised her eyebrows at the notion.

'I'm sorry to have kept you.'

'Don't be silly. It's important. Any time you'd like to talk about Yomi just drop by after school. I'm here for at least an hour marking homework.'

'Thanks,' he said. 'I will.'

Brigitte reached into her bag, grabbed a pen and notepad and scribbled on it quickly. She tore out the page and handed it to Joseph. 'That's my number,' she said and flushed a little before adding quickly, 'In case it's easier to call.'

That afternoon, Joseph found his fares came slowly, which gave him plenty of time to think about Cyrus's plight. When he eventually picked up a guy who wanted to go to Claremont it was the excuse he needed. After he dropped the fare, Joseph drove five more blocks until he reached the Meteor Club, Ray's hangout. The club lay in a part of town he would normally have avoided, with the old grey building sandwiched between a coin-in-the-slot peep show and a Titty bar on one side and a derelict warehouse on the other. The Titty bar had a neon sign that changed intermittently. First it offered Nude Girls then it promised Live Girls. It didn't say anything about Dead Girls, thought Joseph ruefully.

Visiting the Meteor was an important first step, for Joseph had made a decision. He was going to investigate the death of Tina Ferreira. It was the only way he knew to help Cyrus clear his name. They went back too far for Joseph to stand by and do nothing while his oldest and dearest friend went to jail. Joseph had not been near a murder enquiry since he left Lagos and, though he was sure he retained the instincts of a detective, this would be nothing like Nigeria. He would have no choice but to do this one on his own. There would be no back-up and he would have none of the authority his former status as a law-enforcement officer afforded him, so it would be far more dangerous if things went wrong. These days he did not even own a gun.

Joseph parked up, prayed his cab would still be there when he returned and went inside the Meteor.

The place was dark and oppressive, with no light admitted from the outside even during the day. The bar was almost empty, except for a couple of hard-core drinkers in a corner, the kind of men who can't get through their day without a livener at regular intervals, and a burly man reading a newspaper by the door. He didn't have a drink in front of him and that, combined with his size, made him look as if he was on the payroll. Joseph went up to the bar just as the girl behind it wandered away on some errand. It was then he finally noticed the strikingly beautiful but hard-faced young black girl who was seated on a stool at the end of the bar, nursing what could have been a vodka and tonic. Joseph did a double take, for she looked very like Apara when she was that age. She was younger than his wife of course, but there was no mistaking the resemblance between this girl and the young woman he met all those years ago.

'She'll be back,' she said, meaning the bar girl, her words heavier with the accent of Africa than America, 'but Tyler ain't working today.'

'Okay,' he said cautiously, for she had clearly confused him with somebody else.

'I can hook you up with one of the other girls,' she offered.

'That's okay.'

The girl seemed surprised by this and she took a closer look at Joseph. 'You been here before?' she asked.

'No.'

She seemed to squint at him through the gloom. 'Oh, so you ain't he.' She said it almost absentmindedly, as she realised her error.

'I don't know, but I'm not looking to hook up with anybody.'

The girl gave Joseph a look that travelled all the way up then back down him. 'Pity,' she said with a little smile. 'What are you looking for?'

'Just a drink.'

'Nobody comes in here for a drink,' she said as if he was deluded. 'What else you wanting?'

Joseph smiled. 'Like I say, a drink, maybe two. A conversation with a beautiful lady like you is a bonus.'

'Get the fuck out of here,' she said, laughing. 'Where the fuck you come from talking like that?' she asked, as if the answer could be Mars.

'Highbridge,' he answered. 'Before that, Lagos.'

'Jeez, you kidding?' she seemed to soften at this. 'I came over from Abuja when I was fifteen.' Then she hollered through to the back room, 'Hey! Get this guy a drink!'

'What's your name?' he asked.

'Maritza.' She gave him a crooked little smile when he offered his hand. 'You English or something?' She giggled at the formality but leaned over and took his hand, giving Joseph an uninhibited view of a full figure in a tight, white T-shirt with a plunging neckline. Her arms were bare and his eyes were drawn to a vivid tattoo on her forearm of a snake with green scales and a protruding tongue. It looked like something out of a voodoo ritual.

The bar girl finally appeared and Joseph realised why she had gone out the back. She was now dressed in a tiny, black bikini, an unusual outfit for Claremont in the winter but he guessed the guys who spent their time here expected it.

'I'm Joseph,' he said. 'I've only been in the country a few months. Since then I've been drinking Irish whisky like it comes free with the welfare.' He had always found a lie was easier if it was based on the truth. 'Only thing that ever gets me off to sleep these days. Hope you don't mind if I have some of my drug of choice? I see you got Bushmills.'

This kind of talk she understood. 'Sure, knock yourself out.'

'Join me. We'll drink to home. What do you say, Maritza?'

She shrugged. 'If you're buying.' She said it like she didn't care one way or the other, but at the same time she adjusted her hair, sweeping it back out of her eyes with her hand.

The bar girl poured them both a drink then left them to it. He figured Maritza had to be some sort of buffer between Ray, or whoever owned this joint, and the girls he had just been offered so casually. He wondered what Maritza got out of the deal. She had the looks of a model but there was something damaged about her, Joseph could sense it. Why else would she be sitting in a dump like this? She was taking a risk as it would be her who would be pulled in if the cops raided the place. Ray probably viewed a little prostitution on the side as a good earner while he was spreading drugs all over the South Bronx. Joseph took his time, sipped his drink slowly and traded stories of the old country with Maritza. This brought her out of herself and the conversation became easier.

After a while she asked, 'So what do you do?'

'Drive a cab. You work here full time?'

'Just the day shift usually, some nights.' She became self-conscious as she added, 'Like tonight. But I could leave here at six.'

There was a clear invitation in the words. He glanced at the clock behind her. 'Not long to go now then?'

'It'll just fly by,' she said.

It was a tempting thought. Other guys would just leave this bar with Maritza and forget all their troubles for a while but not Joseph. Who was he trying to kid? 'Well I hope you have a real nice evening, Maritza, either way,' he said.

She didn't even bother to disguise the look of disgust. Instead she ordered herself another drink without asking him if he wanted one, too. Joseph knew what their flirtation had been about – it had been a long time since he had been with a woman and the ache he was feeling in his heart and deep in the pit of his stomach right now was simple loneliness, nothing more. Maritza was beautiful, there was no denying it, but maybe there was more to it than that. She so reminded him of Apara in those early days, beautiful yet sad and needing someone to rescue her from a life she hated so. But that was Apara and this girl wasn't his problem.

Maritza pointed at his empty glass. 'You done?'

'I'd better be, got to drive.'

'Oh yeah, your cab, I almost forgot.' She said it in the cruel, disparaging way of a woman who has been scorned and Joseph accepted it in that light. He knew he would have to leave but he hadn't made any progress.

'Ray still run this place?' he asked as non-chalantly as he could.

'Who wants to know?' she asked, and before he could even think of a reply she walked away.

Joseph realised he had overstepped the mark. Bringing up Ray with no preamble had been a clumsy mistake. He finished the last dregs of his drink, stepped down off the stool and walked slowly to the door.

The man at the table in front of him stopped reading his newspaper and was looking at him suspiciously. Joseph decided to walk right by him as if he didn't have a care in the world.

'Where are you going, bro?' called a voice behind him. 'What's your hurry all of a sudden?'

The burly man eased his enormous frame out from behind the table and blocked Joseph's path to the door. Joseph turned and was confronted by three men who had emerged from a back room. Two were large, heavy-set Dominican guys, who could easily be nightclub doormen. The third was a thin, weasel-faced black man with a pockmarked face and filthy dreadlocks. Though he seemed half the size of the other men, Joseph guessed he was their leader and instinctively knew that this was the most dangerous man in the room.

The dreadlocked newcomer opened his

mouth to reveal crooked, yellow teeth like broken tombstones. 'I hear you looking for Ray. Now why you be doing that?'

7

'Sit,' said Ray and, before he could obey, Joseph was pressed down into a chair by one of Ray's heavies.

He had been dragged into the middle of a large, windowless storeroom. The only light came from a solitary bulb with no shade that hung down from the ceiling above him and a bank of CCTVs against one wall, blinking out constantly changing images from all corners of the club. You couldn't get in or out of the Meteor without being picked up on one of these monitors, but Joseph knew how easy it was to make inconvenient footage disappear, along with any man who walked in here uninvited and asked for Ray. He knew he would have to think fast.

The heavy, who looked to Joseph like he had just escaped from the Bronx Zoo, leaned over him and pressed two enormous hands firmly down on Joseph's shoulders to emphasise he should not try to move. He found himself looking up into hate-filled eyes that peered down at him from a lopsided face, one half of which was disfigured by scar tissue. Joseph had seen the results of many a bar-room brawl and it looked to him as if someone had smashed a glass bottle into this man's face then twisted the jagged pieces to cause maximum damage.

Another of Ray's men turned and locked the door behind them just as loud music started up from the bar. Had Maritza thoughtfully increased the volume to disguise the beating he was about to receive? Joseph glanced about him. There was a small, wooden table and four chairs containing the remnants of a day's discussion on the business of dealing drugs and pimping women. Cigarette butts filled the ashtrays, Styrofoam cups competed for space alongside beer bottles in an overflowing wastebasket. There wasn't even a back door.

Slowly and deliberately, Ray sat down in the chair opposite Joseph then he took a gun out of his jacket and carefully placed it on the table between them. Light caught the silver Glock automatic pistol and it gleamed beneath the bare bulb.

'So, what have we got here?' asked Ray of his minions. 'Another one of them undercover cops looking to make a name for himself by trying to take down old Ray, huh? You sure picked the wrong guy to come round asking about, bro'.' He turned to the second heavy, a black man with a face like an unsuccessful boxer. 'See if he's wearing a wire.'

Joseph was hauled to his feet once more and every inch of his frame patted down.

'He's clean.' The man took Joseph's wallet and threw it to Ray who caught it one-handed. 'No guns, no knives, no wire.' Joseph was pressed back into his seat once more.

'Good thing, too,' said Ray. 'So what's your story, cop?' He took a cigarette and lit it, then let his chair lean back until two of its legs were off the ground.

Joseph tried to look small. Harmless and small. From the moment he had been forced into the back room, he'd been thinking about his cover story. 'I don't know any cops and I don't know what it is you do exactly, Mr Ray, but I do know you've been hiring drivers from my cab company, you pay well and I need the work.'

'Oh yeah? What kind of work is that?'

'Whatever there is.'

'You say you don't know what I do to earn my corn?' challenged Ray. 'But I bet you got a good idea.'

'Maybe I do at that,' said Joseph and he looked Ray directly in the eye, 'but I figure it's nobody's business but his how a man earns a living. I drive a cab all day long and it don't pay shit. When I came to America I knew the law. I did everything by the book.

I got my Green Card, paid my social security and signed up to drive a Crown Victoria cab with a medallion. Know where it got me? My boss cheats me out of whatever I don't already give to the revenue. My fares get picked up by unlicensed drivers who don't pay a cent in tax or leasing costs. I live in a project with my son that's got mould growing on every wall. I don't know what's more dangerous; the place we live in or the school he's got to go to every day. So I've been thinking, man there has got to be more than this. I know there is. I've seen it and I want some.'

Once again Joseph had chosen the lie that was closest to the truth. He reasoned that a man like Ray might believe the petty resentments of how a low pay, thankless grind could disillusion an honest man and turn him bad, particularly when there was so-called easy money to be had elsewhere.

'I ain't no hard man, no gangster, but I learned enough to know that the law is not always on the side of the working man, you hear what I'm saying? Sometimes you got to go with the flow when you need more dough. I got to make some dollars to get me and my son out of here and I am prepared to do whatever it takes, whatever it takes.' He let the last words hang in the air while Ray stared at him intently.

Ray was acting like he'd barely heard

Joseph. Instead he was fiddling with one of the two gold rings on his right hand, turning them round his fingers. 'Shit,' he said eventually. 'I watched you come in here and you even walk like a cop.'

Joseph laughed. 'Well there's nothing I can do about that, but I ain't too concerned 'cos I know if you're really hiring, you'll check me out.'

'And what will I find?'

'You'll find a guy works for the United cab company down on Jerome Avenue. Guys all know me; they'll tell you about Joseph Soyinka, he's on the level.'

'That a fact?' sneered Ray. 'You just a regular guy looking to support his family? Doesn't do drugs, bang whores, or throw his pay cheque away on a poker game. Probably even goes to church?'

'I work on Sundays,' said Joseph. 'When you check me out you'll see I work every hour there is down at that damn cab company 'cept sleeping time. What sort of cop would go undercover driving a cab for a year then come up out of the blue and ask you for work? What kind of cop'd do that?'

'A fucking clever one,' said Ray, and his men both laughed dutifully, though he spoke it like he didn't really believe it. 'So you ain't a cop?' he asked in a deadpan drawl.

'Fuck no,' said Joseph with a big smile.

'They were the reason I left Lagos in the first place.'

Ray nodded. 'You are right, Joseph.' He took a long drag on his cigarette while he weighed up his captive. 'We'll check you out and if you are lying to old Ray, I'm gonna slice that shit-eating grin right off of your face. You got that?'

'I got it.'

'If you stack up, maybe we'll talk. If you don't I'm gonna come find you. Then I'll cut you into small pieces and feed you to my dogs.'

In that moment Ray looked as if he truly enjoyed administering violence and was probably very good at it. He made an almost imperceptible gesture with his hand and the heavy with the scarred face immediately walked over to the door and opened it to show Joseph he should be on his way.

'Get his phone number.'

'Thanks,' Joseph said and he walked slowly from the room, heart pounding.

Outside the room, Joseph gave his number to the heavy then looked towards the bar as he crossed the floor. Maritza avoided his gaze. He didn't really blame her. Joseph doubted she relished handing him in like that, but she was probably too scared of Ray to contemplate anything else.

Then his eye was drawn to a small group

that must have arrived while he was in the back room. The four new arrivals were talking animatedly at a table, all West Africans like himself. Joseph would have paid them no more attention, but he noticed one of their number had a distinctive brown leather jacket draped over the back of his chair. It was a Belstaff, the same colour and make as the one he had seen on the news that morning. Back then it had been used to hide the identity of the brave and traumatised witness to the killing of young Tina Ferreira. Strangely enough, the man seemed fully recovered from his ordeal now, as he laughed and joked with his friends. There were no outside signs of trauma as he enjoyed his drink.

The presence of this man in Ray's bar could hardly be a coincidence. His link to the ruthless drug dealer who had good reason to frame Cyrus was enough for Joseph to seriously doubt his portrayal by the police, as an innocent caught up in gangland war. Something was definitely not right and Joseph was convinced Cyrus's recent troubles had a lot to do with Ray and the man with the Belstaff jacket.

As Joseph walked past the small group, the man with the leather jacket looked up and caught his eye but Joseph did not look away. He wanted to remember that face. By the time he reached the door, he realised he had been sweating so hard his shirt was stuck to him. All the while he had talked with Ray he knew if he said the wrong thing just once, if he overstretched his hand even a little, he would never leave that dark storeroom alive. A man like Ray might think twice about murdering a detective with a badge, but killing Joseph wouldn't give him a moment's concern. Joseph crossed the road and walked quickly away from the Meteor.

'You got to have a real good eye to do this kind of work and mine ain't good for shit no more,' said Marjorie dolefully as she peered uncertainly at her handiwork. 'It's one of the first things to go, Joseph when you gets old, your eyes.' Then she snorted, 'I don't care what any motherfucker says, there ain't no good thing I can tell you 'bout getting old.'

'Weak eyes or not, you've done a hell of a better job than I ever could,' said Joseph, studiously ignoring the old lady's foul mouth.

Marjorie held Yomi's blazer higher so she could catch the light that shone through her apartment window and squinted at the little stitches she'd made. Marjorie was a survivor, a seventy-nine year old who liked to tell everybody she had the heart of a teenager. Unfortunately she had arthritis more in keeping with a woman of her years. Her rooms were on the same floor as Joseph and Yomi, so they looked out for each other. She would sit with Yomi when Joseph had to go out and he knew he could always come to her for repair jobs, like the blazer that she had somehow managed to coax back from the dead. In return, Joseph ran errands, picked up groceries and looked in on Marjorie, which she appreciated more than she cared to admit, for she had been broken into on more than one occasion.

'It's lucky I ain't got nothing worth stealing,' she said when it happened for the third time.

Finally Marjorie was satisfied with the job and nodded to indicate the work was passable. 'Well, he ain't wearing it to the prom so it'll do for now.'

'Thank you, Marjorie.'

'Oh, you don't have to thank me none.' They were sitting in her little front room and, as usual, the radio was on low in the background. It was some phone-in show but she didn't seem to be listening. She probably just liked to have it on so she could hear another human voice. 'I'm glad to do it for you after all you do for me, fetching and carrying all the time.'

'That's what friends are for,' said Joseph. 'In fact I did a little fetching from the Impala. Picked you up some puff-puffs and chin-chin.' And he handed her a sealed plastic box containing the food. 'Girl down there makes 'em just the way they ought to be made.'

Even though Marjorie had lived all her life in America, she still loved Nigerian food, particularly the sweet things. The puff-puffs were made from sugar, yeast and flour then fried in oil till they were crisp. The chin-chins were Nigerian cookies.

'Oh, Joseph that's real nice of you.' She lifted the lid and took a big sniff before resealing it. 'I'll have that later, it'll be all the better for the waitin'.' Then she climbed to her feet and headed for the part of the room that served as the kitchen. 'I was about to ask how you got that girl from the restaurant to put some of this in a box for me but I guess you banging her, huh?' She cackled to herself when she saw the look of horror on Joseph's face. 'Oh don't you mind old Marjorie, I'm only shitting you. I know you ain't doing it with her.' She put the food away in the refrigerator and turned back to him. 'But you sure as hell should be! Take it from a woman of nearly eighty, Joseph, make the most of your time while you still young 'cos you won't know what you got till it's over. You are a handsome and charming man. You ought to be trying to bang every gal you meet. I'd say they mostly won't mind.'

Joseph shook his head in wonder. 'Marjorie, you know I love you but you cuss like a drunken G.I. Who dragged you up?'

The old woman laughed again. 'Not my momma if that's what you're thinking. That's what happens when you grow up with all brothers like I did. You learn to fight and cuss and spit like a man. Momma died too early to teach me no fancy manners.' She groaned as she sat back down heavily in her chair. 'My Ethan never cared too much either way, god rest him. I'm not like you though, Joseph. The way you talk, I reckon you could charm the birds right down off of the trees.'

Before Joseph could answer, his mobile phone rang shrilly. 'Excuse me,' he said and stood up to take the call.

'See what I mean,' she said as he walked away from her chair. '"Excuse me".' And she mimicked his broad, well-spoken way.

'Hello,' said Joseph cautiously when he was happy Marjorie was out of earshot.

A chill and menacing voice answered him. 'It's Ray. We checked you out, so now we talking.'

'Okay,' he said cautiously.

'Friend of mine's gonna call you with the address of a warehouse. You be there tonight at one and we'll see what we shall see, you in?'

'Yeah,' answered Joseph. He knew he was being tested but there were few clues in Ray's words. He waited for more information but instead there was a click and the drug dealer was gone.

'That your work, honey?' asked Marjorie.

'That's right.' He knew she was only making conversation but Joseph felt uneasy discussing the matter with the old lady.

'You got to go out again tonight?'

'I got to go out again tonight,' he admitted, feeling incredibly tired all of a sudden.

'There's no rest for the wicked,' she said laughing. 'That's what they say.'

As Joseph edged the car further north along Harlem River Drive, he started to feel an increased sense of anxiety. Did he really know what he was doing here? Had he bitten off more than he could safely chew? Joseph had started out that afternoon with one clear purpose – to investigate the murder of Tina Ferreira in order to prove his friend innocent of her brutal killing. Now, as he drove closer to the docks, he realised he had taken an irreversible step. He was about to pose as a drugs courier and that seemed like a very dangerous game indeed, even to him. But how else was he ever going to get close to Ray and find out what was really going on?

Back at the house with Marjorie and Yomi, Joseph had begun to convince himself nothing was going to happen that night or any other night when Ray's associate finally called. When the phone chirruped into life he'd answered it on the second ring.

'This Joseph?'

'Uh-huh.'

'Take down an address,' said a deep voice he had never heard before. Joseph wrote down the details of a site in Yonkers on the back of an old envelope. 'Be standing outside warehouse number eleven at 1.00 a.m., man gonna be delivering you a package there, just like DHL only you don't got to sign. Take the package and bring it to Ray at the Meteor. Got that?'

'Sure,' and the line went dead.

Joseph knocked on Yomi's door. 'I've got to go out on a job later.'

'Okay,' his son called back through the door.

'It's an airport run, so I'll be two or three hours.' Yomi didn't bother to answer. 'Make sure you finish your homework before bed.'

It had crossed Joseph's mind to tell Eddie what he was doing, so that at least one person would know where he was going and on whose bidding, but he knew the old cop would never understand the risk Joseph was taking for his friend. Eddie would probably try and talk him out of it.

He parked the cab by an enormous, corrugated-iron building, surrounded by a number of others that looked exactly the same in the gloom. It was pitch dark down here by the water level, the only light coming from some way off, where a number of small boats were moored. Joseph had to squint at the paper to read the number of the warehouse once more and then he checked his map. This had to be the place. He climbed from the cab and immediately stepped into a deep puddle that sent cold water up over the laces of his shoes. He cursed and the sound of his own voice made the place seem even more lonely and imposing. The puddle had been virtually invisible in the darkness and he was forced to pick his away carefully across the road between the warehouses, to avoid more water and some deep and treacherous cracks in the concrete.

Joseph found the warehouse, its number written in white paint on the door. It was the correct spot alright but he was early so now he was forced to wait, blowing on his hands to keep out the worst of the cold, which cut through Joseph's inadequate jacket and chilled his bones. Steam came from his mouth in clouds when he breathed out and he stamped his feet on the ground to keep the blood flowing but he continued to wait by the warehouse door like a sentry on guard duty.

He didn't know what to expect. Would the warehouse suddenly open from the inside and his contact emerge or would he sidle up to greet him from out of the impenetrable darkness. He was forced to concede that someone could be watching him just a few yards away and he would still not know anything about it.

Suddenly Joseph started, as the sound of an engine reached him. The noise was still some way off and a little high-pitched, but instinct told him it was linked to his cold vigil. As it drew nearer, he realised it was a motorcycle engine and, sure enough, one of those powerful 750cc Japanese motorbikes came into view at the opposite end of the docks then roared towards him. At first Joseph thought its rider was going to mow him down and he almost made a run for it. He had to force himself to stand his ground. As the bike drew nearer it suddenly veered to one side and it looked as if the rider would be thrown from it but he was merely bringing the motorbike expertly to a halt.

The rider dismounted with practiced ease then walked quickly towards Joseph without removing the dark helmet he wore. This sinister spectre marching towards him in black leathers and motorcycle helmet was an alarming sight. Wasn't it common for hit men to carry out jobs on motorbikes so they could flee the murder scene quickly? Didn't they also keep their helmets in place to mask their identities? What could he do down here in the dark, unarmed and unaided, if the mystery man suddenly pulled out a gun and shot him?

Before anxiety got the better of him, Joseph noticed the man was carrying a small, brown satchel in his gloved hand. As he got closer, the man spoke, his voice muffled by the helmet's visor. 'Are you Joseph?'

Joseph nodded and the satchel was thrust out to him. He took it gingerly and the man added, 'take this to Ray at the Meteor.'

Without uttering another word or waiting for an answer, the man turned, walked back to his motorbike, climbed on it and sped off. Joseph was left standing there alone, staring down at the package full of drugs in his hands.

Driving through the late-night traffic with a contraband cargo was an unsettling experience. If Ray wanted to frame someone he did not trust, what better way than to give Joseph some drugs and set the cops on him as soon as he was back on the road. Joseph thought this notion through and dismissed it. If Ray tried to frame him, Joseph would be inclined to tell the cops it was all a set-up planned by Ray and they might just believe the cab driver over the presumably known drug dealer. In any case, planting real drugs on somebody in sufficient quantity was an expensive business that would surely never be wasted on a lowly driver. Ray could just as easily have told Joseph there was no work going right now and that would have been the end of the matter.

Strange to admit it but he was actually pleased when the bright neon sign that hung above the door of the Meteor came into view. There was a short queue of rough-looking young clubbers that stretched to the corner of the building but Joseph walked right up to one of the burly doormen and announced, 'I got a delivery for Ray.'

The doorman recognised Joseph. He was the same guy who had patted him down when he was looking for a wire earlier that afternoon. He waved him into the building.

As Joseph entered, the noise, heat and acrid smell of sweat, beer and effects smoke hit him. What a contrast to the sedate scene of earlier. It was a young crowd and they filled every space. Gangsta rap blared from enormous speakers positioned in each corner and, as he crossed the room, it morphed into the latest from Kanye West. An area had been cleared in the centre of the floor and two young, white girls dressed in black had taken centre stage, while they threw themselves around this makeshift dance floor with an abandon that could only be drug fuelled. Occasionally they barged into other people and were shoved back into the centre, like pinballs trapped in a machine. A large, multi-headed spotlight whirled above them sending crazy silhouetted shapes against the walls. Most of the crowd were drinking from bottles of expensive imported beer and shouting at each other so they could be heard above the din.

Joseph tried to ease his way across the floor, but found his progress blocked by youths too high to really notice him. They duly parted once he exerted a little force. It took him a time to reach the bar, but once he was there he immediately caught Maritza's eye. She acted as if their earlier conversation hadn't happened and instead pointed to the door he had passed through earlier. Joseph noticed that a huge, shaven-headed black man guarded the door. He wore a tight, black T-shirt, barely containing muscles that bulged so prominently they could only be the result of hours spent in the gym or a prison recreation yard. He was soon joined by an other man in a black leather coat with a tattoo that covered his neck and stretched up half the back of his head. 'Bar codes for criminals,' was how Eddie described them, adding, 'the only thing a Tatt guarantees them is future iden-tification. They never learn.' Joseph started to wonder if they bought their scary, muscle-men clothes from the same store. All Ray's men looked like they'd been hired from central casting. Was this a case of hard men dressing like guys from the movies, or did film stars try to emulate the latest look on the street?

'You're expected. I have to take you over there!' Maritza shouted the words so she could be heard above the din. There was something in the way she said 'I have to' that made it clear the task would give her no pleasure. Hell hath no fury, thought Joseph.

After a moment or two of shoving, they reached the door. Maritza was instantly admitted and Joseph went next, the shaven-headed man followed. As he walked into the room, he was immediately blocked by two more large men and patted down once again. Another pair of men watched Joseph intently from a distance. Ray's crew had all been chosen for the same reason. If you could scare and intimidate, you were in.

Ray was watching from the table nearby and Maritza joined him. 'You have something that belongs to us.' Ray glanced at the satchel, and Joseph held it up. 'Open it,' he commanded.

Joseph did as he was told. In the satchel was a large, clear-film bag of grainy white powder, heavy enough to have a street value of thousands of dollars.

'Now you listen to me and you listen good,' said Ray. 'I don't trust you. You got cop written all over your face. Shit, I can even smell the cop on you.' He tilted his head back and sniffed the air ostentatiously.

'Man, you reek of it.' Joseph stayed silent. 'You got some talking to do, boy. Otherwise I'm going to save myself the trouble of even getting to know you. My boys will take you out the back door and you'll disappear. No one will ever see your face again. You'd better believe it. So convince me, man.' Ray looked at him watch. 'You got one minute.'

Joseph didn't say a word. Instead he let the empty satchel drop to the floor, took the bag of white powder in both hands and tore it open. Baxter opened his mouth in wonder at the gesture, then his eyes widened in astonishment. Joseph turned the bag upside down and allowed all the precious powder to pour out in one steady and continuous white stream, until every grain had been lost to the filthy floor of the Meteor.

8

One of the heavies, with a scarred face, immediately leapt to his feet and advanced on Joseph. 'You motherfucker!' he screamed as he cocked the pistol and pressed it hard against the side of Joseph's head almost knocking him off his feet.

'Talk fast,' said Ray.

'Do you think I'm a fool?' asked Joseph.

'There's got to be three kilos of white powder here and coke ain't cheap. Are you seriously expecting me to believe you are going to give that amount of blow to a man you don't trust? A man who smells like a cop? I don't think so.'

Ray watched him intently, weighing Joseph's fate in his hands. Finally, he spoke very quietly, 'Put the gun down, Heroll.'

The scar-faced heavy acted as if he hadn't heard his boss. There was a wild fury in his eyes. This time the single word was hissed and it was a warning. 'Heroll.' Reluctantly, Heroll lowered the gun and took a step back.

There was no one behind him, but Ray tilted his head back as if he was talking to a ghost, 'Did you get that?'

'I did,' said a deep, metallic, disembodied voice coming out of an unseen transmitter, before adding 'I'm coming down.'

A moment later, the door opened and a newcomer walked confidently into the room. He surveyed Joseph with interest. He was a tall, broad, black figure in his early thirties, a sharp dresser, wearing what Joseph would have described as a "thousand dollar suit", perfectly tailored to fit his bulky frame. His face had a healthy gleam that spoke of good grooming, fine living and, most importantly, the avoidance of his own product. The new man looked at the pile of bogus cocaine on the floor, then squinted at Joseph as if he couldn't quite believe his eyes.

He smiled and shook his head. 'Well you are either the stupidest motherfucker that ever lived or you've got balls made out of fucking Kryptonite or something. You know how close you just came to dying?'

'You knew the drugs were fake?' said Joseph, assuming the man to be Ray's boss.

'Yeah, and so did Ray but Heroll didn't.' The big man began to laugh. He roared like he'd just heard the funniest thing imaginable. Scarface scowled at Joseph, resentful at being called off by his master. 'Heroll didn't,' repeated the big man, as he struggled to contain himself, and Joseph finally realised just how near to death he had come.

'I'm TJ and you might just talk yourself into a job with balls that size.' The big man stood and offered Joseph his hand. Joseph took it and his own hand was enclosed by a powerful grip.

'TJ? That's what I call you?' he asked, hoping for more of a clue to the man's identity.

TJ nodded. 'That or just plain "boss".'

He motioned for Joseph to sit down and ordered Maritza to fetch some drinks. 'What will you have, Joseph?' he asked.

'I know what he drinks,' she said and stomped away.

'Guess you already made an impression on her,' said TJ. 'What do you think of Maritza? You like her?'

Joseph was deliberately evasive. 'I don't think she likes me.'

TJ snorted. 'That ain't no bad thing. Maritza is my brother's lady. He away right now so I got to look out for her and make sure she don't get distracted by no tall, handsome strangers. You want a little pussy, Joseph? Maybe you get some once you proved yourself, if you do the right thing by us, but you stay away from Maritza, you got that?' Joseph nodded, but stayed silent as TJ walked behind him and disappeared from view. TJ leaned forwards till he was close to Joseph's ear and when he spoke his voice was low. 'You understand the reason for our little test. I got to be sure about you. Whenever I make someone an offer of employment, *especially* then, I have to he real sure. I need to know they aren't going to double-cross me, run off with my product, call the cops, be the cops. There's so much to think about.'

'I understand.'

'I hope you do and don't mind Baxter,' TJ was referring to Ray, so that was the gangster's name, Ray Baxter. 'He may look like a nasty guy to you but I see him as a total fucking psycho.' And he laughed at his own joke. Baxter didn't take it well. TJ walked over to Baxter and slapped him on the shoulder. 'Between you and me, that's why I keep him around. You see, I'm at war, Joseph. Who would you want on your side in a war? A nice guy or a man like Baxter here?'

Joseph glanced at Baxter, who stared straight back at him with barely contained fury. 'Oh, I'd want him on my side, definitely.'

'Yes, you would,' said TJ. 'You seem to understand my business pretty well for a civilian so let's cut the small talk, shall we? I got a big deal going down in a while. I need good men, men I can trust, who'll help me to distribute my product just as soon as it hits the ground. No one wants that kind of gear lying around for long.' TJ took out an expensive, calfskin wallet and extracted a one-hundred-dollar bill. 'Take it,' he ordered. Joseph reached out to take the money and TJ immediately took it back and held it out of reach. 'This is for your trouble today but it could be just the beginning. You show up when I tell you and play your part like a good soldier and there's a lot more where that came from. For a man like you it'll seem like a whole lot of greenback for a day's work.'

'Damn right,' agreed Joseph, and for a moment he allowed himself to imagine what he could buy with a good deal of undeclared income. A new cab for one thing. Of course, he could just as easily get twenty years in prison instead, particularly when the man offering this easy money was a hardcore drug dealer.

'So you trust me now?' smiled Joseph.

'Not yet. I trust you about as far as I trust anyone I just met, but I think we might be okay with you, Joseph. Remember, you look like a cop. It's always the ones who don't look like cops who get sent undercover.'

'I never thought of that.'

'It's a fact. If we call you, and I do mean *if*, we'll start you off small so we know you're okay. You'd be driving one of my guys around for a while first. Would you be interested in something like that?'

'I sure would.'

'Good.' He handed Joseph the one-hundred-dollar bill. 'Just one last thing and I am only going to tell you this the one time so you'd better listen up.' He gave Joseph the most benign of smiles. 'If you do come and work for us, don't ever even consider crossing me, Joe. Some have tried. They found out I do not forget and I never forgive. I will kill you but not until you have begged me to do it because, by the time Baxter's finished with you, you'll want death so bad you'll think I am doing you a favour. You got that?' Joseph nodded. 'Good.' TJ was still smiling as Maritza walked back in with a tray of drinks. 'I guess we'll let you know then. Now, what shall we drink to?' TJ took his glass of rum from the tray and raised it. 'How about friendship?' Then he downed it in one gulp.

Joseph was about to start fighting his way back through the crowd when he spotted the guy. Here was a man who seemed out of place. He didn't look high or drunk, he wasn't with anyone else and he didn't have any interest in the sexy girl dancing wildly just a yard in front of him. He wasn't holding a glass and he had kept his jacket on, though the room was hot. He just didn't look right. Instead, he stared straight ahead, focusing his gaze on the door Joseph had just emerged from, which is why Joseph noticed him in the first place. Now why would he be so interested in that room, wondered Joseph. He glanced behind him and saw that TJ, Baxter and Maritza were emerging with their bodyguards but none of them were paying any attention to the crowd around them. Did they feel safe here on their home patch with all their CCTV cameras?

Joseph looked back to where the man had been standing, but he was gone. Suddenly he spotted him again and this time the man was pushing his way through the crowd but he was moving too quickly and shoving too hard for this to be normal. When he came closer, Joseph got a look at his eyes and they were glazed with hatred. He was advancing on TJ and Baxter. The man pushed right through the group on the edge of the bar and, just as he drew alongside Joseph, he pulled out a gun and started to level it on the gangster and his crew who were just yards away. TJ's eyes widened when he realised what was happening and Baxter thrust a hand into his jacket, desperately reaching for his Glock. But it was too late for that.

As the gun came up level with TJ, Joseph stepped in, he took one stride towards the gunman and charged him hard with his shoulder, knocking the man off his feet just as the gun was fired. TJ, Baxter and their men all ducked as the bullet sailed into the wall just above their heads. The gunman crashed to the ground and instantly looked terrified of the retribution that would be coming his way. His only thought now was to get out of there. Fortunately for him, the sound of the gun was enough to send everybody scurrying back out of his way and he turned and fled, leaving the pistol on the ground where it lay just a few feet from him.

'Stop that fuck!' screamed TJ above the din of the music, but the gunman wasn't stopping for anyone. Sheer terror propelled him through the bulk of the man guarding the door. The doorman grabbed at his jacket but only succeeded in tearing it from his back as he stumbled to the floor. When he got to his feet, the gunman had fled.

'Why has he got to do your motherfucking job for you?' demanded TJ of Baxter, once they were all back in the storeroom. 'What do I pay you and your guys for?' He was enraged, and Baxter on the defensive.

'We ain't never seen him before,' Baxter protested.

'Is that all it takes? Fucking greaseballs hire a gunman you ain't met socially and I end up with my fucking head blowed off, if it weren't for this guy.' He jabbed a finger at Joseph. 'Maybe I should make him my right-hand man since he seems to know more about protecting me than you do.'

'Which bothers me, now I come to think about it,' answered Baxter and he scowled resentfully at Joseph. 'How'd you know that cocksucker was going to pull a gun?'

'He was staring at the door when I walked out and he looked kind of stressed, then when you came out he couldn't get to you all quick enough. It didn't surprise me when he pulled a gun.'

'Very convenient...' Baxter began, but TJ cut him short, grabbing the jacket that had been torn from the gunman and throwing it at Baxter.

'Shut the fuck up, Ray!' He turned to the man who had just saved his life. 'You got yourself a job, Joseph.'

When Joseph called round, he was surprised to see the door to Eddie's apartment ajar. When he'd been a detective that usually meant one thing, a break-in, and Eddie wasn't the sort to leave his door open in this neighbourhood. Joseph tapped tentatively on the wood and it swung inwards a little.

'It's open,' called Eddie.

'I can see that,' said Joseph as he walked in. 'Who you expecting? Cameron Diaz?'

'No, I had to cancel her,' answered Eddie without looking up, 'she cooks a lousy breakfast.' Eddie was hunched over his ancient turntable, fussing with an old LP record.

Joseph closed the door behind him and almost tripped over three brown-paper bags filled with groceries that had been left on the floor. They were the reason for Eddie's brief journey out into the cold that morning. Eddie lowered the needle and an all-too-familiar voice began to croon through the speakers, filling the room with mournful song.

Joseph knew Eddie had an inordinate pride in his stereo. It had been lovingly assembled with expensive equipment from specialist hi-fi dealers many years before the advent of CDs, iPods or MP3s. 'What on earth is that?' he asked his friend teasingly.

'That is Francis Albert Sinatra, you goddammed philistine, and may god rot you for saying it.'

'I know who's doing the singing. I was referring to the pile of junk you were playing poor Francis Albert on. It looks like something you stole from the flight deck of an aircraft carrier back in World War Two.'

'This is a work of art,' said Eddie proudly. 'I will not tell you how much it cost me in dollars-green, way back when, but it was a lot. Maggie almost blew a fuse when she found out and she didn't even know the half of it. But it was worth every penny to hear Francis Albert the way he ought to be heard.'

'Mmm, I'll take your word for it. I prefer something more modern myself and you'd get a better sound quality on the computer down at Yomi's school these days.'

Eddie pulled a face like he'd just eaten something rotten. 'Oh please, that's no way to hear music. That's like dating a woman on a computer? Me? I'd rather have the real thing.'

'Tell that to poor Cameron. So, you realise your door was wide open, right?'

'I was getting round to closing it. I like a bit of Sinatra while I put the damned groceries away. You okay with that?'

'Yep.' Eddie fell silent for a moment while

Francis Albert told them both just how bewitched, bothered and bewildered some girl had made him.

'No one can carry a toon like Sinatra,' said Eddie wistfully, 'especially a torch song. I'm talking about the Capitol years, of course.'

'Of course.' Joseph's tone was mocking. Eddie pointed at his shopping. 'Make yourself useful while you're ruining my morning. Put those bags up on the counter top to save me bending down for 'em. Do that small thing and I'll let you make us both a coffee.'

'Gee, thanks,' deadpanned Joseph.

'So what's on your mind?'

Joseph lifted up the groceries and started to prepare the coffee. 'You ever come across a guy called TJ while you were in the job?'

Eddie thought for a moment and shook his head. 'Should I have?'

'I hear he's a player in the local drug trade. Wondered if it meant anything to you.'

'No,' said Eddie sharply, 'and I'm surprised it means something to you. Why the sudden interest in your friendly local drug dealer? You ain't a detective no more, Joseph, you forgotten that?'

'I've not forgotten.' Joseph was unsure how much to reveal to his friend. He knew Eddie was no fool and would not be easily fobbed off with a lie but he wasn't going to tell him how he'd barged a hit man out of the way to save that local drug dealer. Even Joseph wasn't sure why he had acted that way, except it was always an instinctive reaction to stop anyone from taking a life. Besides it would be no use to Cyrus if TJ, a man seemingly at the centre of all his troubles, was shot dead. Joseph had been there before in Lagos. 'I've been thinking about what happened to Cyrus, looking into it. Turns out those courier jobs he was mixed up in were for a man who goes by the name of TJ. That's all I got, just the initials TJ.'

'Be careful, Joseph, you ain't got a badge no more and you ain't got a gun. It's dangerous enough to investigate a man like this when you got both and it helps to have the backing of the entire NYPD, but you're a one-man band, which means even the cops'll think you're a pain in the ass. You wind up dead, they'll just shrug and say stupid mother had it coming.'

'Thanks.'

'I'm just telling it like it is. When I first joined the force an old hand told me "make sure when you retire there is no such thing as unfinished business. You turn your back on it all and walk away, no vendettas, no personal stuff, no dumb-ass freelance operations, because that's how you get yourself killed".' He was right. I left a good deal of incomplete stuff in New Jersey, but I never looked back, not once. Seems to me you could do well to remember that. You're a civilian now, got to look out for yourself and so has Cyrus, I'm sorry to say.'

'Maybe you're right but he's my friend. What would you do if it was one of your old police buddies who was in trouble? Just forget about them? I doubt that and I know Cyrus didn't do it.' Eddie raised an eyebrow. 'I know it,' repeated Joseph emphatically.

'What do you know? A week ago you'd have sworn on a stack of bibles that he was no drug dealer. These days no one knows anyone, Joseph, believe me.'

There did not seem anything to add to that gloomy pronouncement so the two men took their coffee, letting Sinatra provide the background music while they sat in silence.

Eventually Joseph broke it. 'This TJ, he's a Dominican, like those guys you investigated across the river. When was that?'

''Bout three years ago. The gang leader was lucky. We couldn't get the drug charges to stick, had to settle for assault with a deadly weapon. He got five when it should have been life for all the shitty things he did.' Eddie seemed perturbed by the memory. 'Basically we lucked out and fucked up. Wish we could have done things differently at the time, but we didn't and that's all there is to it.'

'What was his name?'

Eddie thought for a moment. 'Jakes, Alphonse Jakes.'

'Jakes,' said Joseph. 'Now there's a thought. There can't be hundreds of Dominicans in positions of power in the New York drug scene. I wonder if TJ is related to AJ. Maybe he relocated the family business from New Jersey to the South Bronx.'

'Careful, Joseph,' warned Eddie. 'This is a world you couldn't possibly understand.'

Later, in Joseph's apartment for supper, Yomi sat on the carpet manically jabbing his thumbs at a games console that was rigged up to the TV, while Eddie joined Joseph at the table to talk over the day's events. The boy was completely engrossed in the action, which was noisily erupting from the screen.

Eddie asked, 'You in the mood for a game later or are you too tired to get your butt kicked?'

'I'm never too tired to beat you at chess, Eddie. It's only our games and the whisky that get me off to sleep at all. Can't seem to get my head down without at least one of them these days, but let's wait till Yomi's finished crashing cars and mowing down pedestrians, so I can think straight.'

'I haven't crashed,' said Yomi indignantly.

The games console was strictly second-generation hardware but Yomi didn't seem to mind. Joseph had bought it cheap, along with a handful of games, from another driver who seemed to spend half his life playing on the things and had just spent hundreds of dollars on the latest upgrade. Joseph wondered how his colleague found the time and money to play computer games. He sure as hell couldn't be married, or have kids.

Joseph was preoccupied with thoughts of Cyrus, TJ and Baxter, but he was also watching his son as the boy flung an imaginary Ferrari down a virtual road in the middle of a lurid computerised cityscape. The boy was bouncing up and down in his excitement.

'I'm through the next level. I made it!' he cried.

'Good man,' encouraged Eddie. 'You're driving that car like you stole it.'

Yomi was exulted by his success. He was flinging the car from side to side with considerable skill as it gained speed on the way to the next cyber level. Joseph knew how hard this game was, as he had tried to play it with his son and was forced to give up moments later. He had to admit he was next to useless at these things and was only holding his son back. It would have been hard enough to guide the Ferrari through the crowded city streets but the game had an added complication. Yomi's car was being doggedly pursued by gunmen in another vehicle and they kept shooting at him from its opened windows. He had to dodge bullets as well as other cars and these twin tasks were causing him considerable strain. Joseph watched as Yomi whooped and winced as his car threatened to come flying off the road at any moment.

Just when Yomi thought he had successfully navigated a particularly difficult stage of the game, a new car thundered towards him head-on. The unexpected frontal assault caught his son completely off-guard. Joseph watched as a hand holding an automatic pistol came protruding from the rear window of the black Mustang, a shot was fired and the windscreen of Yomi's car splintered then evaporated as the car swerved, hit another vehicle, spun off the road and turned over, before crashing spectacularly into a wall. The TV froze and the legend "Game Over" appeared on the screen in front of them in big white letters. The deep voice of a computerised gangster told Yomi 'You lose sucker!'

'Oh, where did he come from?' whined Yomi. 'Did you just see that?'

'Yes, I did.' Joseph was up and out of his seat and by his son's side before he could start the game over or turn it off. 'Can you show me that again with the replay thing?'

Yomi was surprised at his father's level of interest. 'Sure, easy.' He hit the replay button on the handset. Joseph watched intently as the black Mustang appeared on the horizon then screeched forwards, the gun was fired, the windscreen shattered and the Ferrari completed its spectacular death roll.

'And again,' he instructed.

The bemused boy pressed replay once more and his father watched the action for a third time. Joseph's eyes never left the screen. When the Ferrari crashed again and the screen froze, he slowly rose to his feet and clenched a fist, slamming it into the palm of his other hand.

'What is it, Dad?'

Joseph looked at his son and announced triumphantly, 'That's it, Yomi. That's it!'

'What's what?' asked Eddie.

But Joseph was already busying himself. He scooped his wallet up from a table, grabbed the keys to the cab and stuffed them in his pocket, then he lifted his jacket from a peg on the back of the front door.

'Dad, where are you going?' asked Yomi.

'I promised you some supper, Eddie.' He was already pulling on his jacket. 'How'd you guys like a Chinese takeout?' Before they could answer he said, 'Great, I'll be back before you know it.' And they watched him hurry out through the door.

'Lord save us, Yomi,' said Eddie. 'I think your dad's finally lost his senses.'

9

The crime scene had been cleared away by now and the road returned to something like normality. The yellow tape that kept back the public had been removed along with the vehicle, and the only clues that there had ever been a killing here at all were the stump of the decapitated streetlamp, its top half having been sawn off and taken away, and a single black mark where the cab had skidded from the road.

Traffic was light when Joseph crossed the rain-drenched road. It was one of those inner-city rat runs that was only ever busy for a couple of hours each morning and evening in the commuter rush, but by now the workers had all struggled home. He stood a few paces back from the scene of the crash and took it in anew, for Yomi's video game had given Joseph some ideas. The pictures he had taken with his battered old Nikon shortly after the crash had been developed a day earlier and they were still in their envelope in his jacket pocket. The first time Joseph looked at them they presented him with no new clues, but now he regarded them with interest once more. He realised the toppled streetlight had been a red herring. To begin with, Joseph had assumed the cab was travelling at speed when the gunman pulled alongside and fired, forcing the driver to career off the road and destroy the lamp in the process. Now he thought back on it he recalled the damage to the cab was really quite minimal and the skid marks in the road were short, meaning the driver must have swerved sharply into the light while still managing to avoid writing off his cab. Joseph could only conclude he was driving slowly, very slowly but why would he do that on a road Joseph knew from experience would normally still be moving briskly, even in the rush hour? Unless he wasn't trying to evade his attacker at all.

Joseph walked up to the damaged street-lamp and peered at it. The metal was thin and the whole structure little more than a hollow tube, easy to break with even the slightest impact. They were probably designed that way to avoid killing drivers who rammed them in a collision, a bit like modern cars with their crumple zones. Hadn't the guy trying to sell Joseph a new Crown Victoria explained to him how new cars might look like they'd been virtually destroyed in accident impacts, but this was actually deliberate? It meant the car took the worst of the impact not the passengers, who quite often got out and walked away from the wreckage. The sight of a streetlamp bent in two had wrong-footed Joseph and, presumably, the NYPD. Both assumed the driver had taken dramatic evasive action to avoid the hit man. In reality, it looked as if he had driven at a virtual snail's pace and the reason finally became clear. The driver of the cab was assisting the assassin and the real target was not him but Tina Ferreira, the so-called accidental victim in this whole sorry mess. The low speed was no accident, designed as it was to give the killer a clean shot at Tina through the cab's front windshield, which meant the killer was probably on foot, just waiting to step out into the street and murder the girl. The shot through the front windshield would have to be accurate, but it would be a far-better smokescreen than a headshot through the passenger side window. This way the world thought Tina wasn't even the intended victim and the killing could be put down as a gang hit gone wrong. It was almost perfect, except Joseph was now starting to unravel the whole thing.

Turning his collar up against the easterly wind, he walked back across the road to the Chinese takeout. The place was quiet now with no traffic jams to encourage hungry commuters through its doors. The same Chinese guy was still working the front till. He was greeted warmly enough, then asked for his order. He waited patiently for his food to be cooked out the back and struck up a conversation, which started on the safe topic of the weather, that eastern wind was such a killer of old people agreed the owner, and migrated through the latest utterances of Hilary Clinton, who he was clearly not a fan of, before Joseph steered it to the murder.

'I see they soon cleared up that mess out there,' he said.

'Yeah, you wouldn't think anything had happened at all, except a pole fall down maybe.'

'I still can't get over you hearing it like that. It must have been terrifying.'

'Well, tell you the truth I didn't know what it was at first. It sounded like a tyre blowing out, then there was this screech of rubber when the poor sap behind the wheel swerved to get away from the guy with the gun.'

'He must have been terrified,' said Joseph.

'Who wouldn't be? Next thing there's another bang as the lamp folds over and I guess it must have clipped the roof of the cab. By the time I looked out it was all but finished.'

'You sure that was the order it happened in?'

The owner seemed defensive. 'Sure, I got ears, haven't I? Why?'

Joseph shrugged. 'No reason, it's just...'

'What?'

'Well, the way I hear it the guy that done the shooting steps straight out in front of the cab and points his gun, then you hear the shot and then you hear the swerve and the skid and the impact with the lamp.'

'So what's your point?'

'Nothing, except if some maniac with a gun stepped out right in front of me, I'd be looking to swerve long before he took aim and fired it, that's all.'

'Mmm, maybe,' agreed the owner. 'Perhaps he was daydreaming, but if it was me I'd have just run the motherfucker down.'

Joseph laughed. 'That might have been the best idea.'

'Hey, if it is him or me, it sure as hell ain't going to be me.'

'Now you're talking.'

A chef handed the owner a large brown bag containing Joseph's order and he popped in a small bag of fortune cookies before passing it across the counter. He must have reflected on Joseph's analysis of the killing for he concluded, 'You're right you know, someone points a gun at me I wouldn't wait around for him to fire. I guess he just didn't see it coming.'

As Joseph drove back to his apartment, he remembered how the glass from the windshield of the cab had fractured but not exploded. There was a clean bullet hole in it from the shot that killed Tina Ferreira. Joseph was no ballistics expert but it indicated to him that the cab had swerved after the shot was fired. The owner of the Chinese restaurant seemed a sharp little guy, who'd probably be a reliable witness, and Joseph was now convinced the cab driver had waited until the shot that killed Tina before he swerved his vehicle quite sedately into the hollow streetlamp. It was then that Joseph remembered Samuel, the old cab driver who had been interviewed by the young detective down at the Impala. What was it he had said? 'If you ask me, it was her job that killed her'.

Joseph's dialled his cab company to see if he could track down Samuel. Not only was he not working that night, he wasn't going to be doing any shifts for the foreseeable future. 'He's gone all the way to Roanoke. Got a sister there that's taken ill. It don't sound too good for her. Won't be back for at least two weeks and he's dropped me right in the shinola. You need any extra shifts, Joseph, you let me know.'

The next morning, Joseph pointed the cab in the general direction of Tremont and set out early to beat the rush hour. It wasn't too hard to find Tina Ferreira's old building as the company logo had featured prominently

144

on the evening news during the reporting of her death. CDS Xenon was a provider of business-to-business IT solutions apparently, which all seemed innocent enough at first glance. Joseph wasn't actually sure what his journey would achieve, but he was intrigued by Samuel's comment and he needed to see where the murdered girl spent her days.

Joseph parked close by and watched the office workers file into a twelve-storey highrise with dirty windows. A little after nine Joseph got out of his cab and walked into the foyer trying to look as if he belonged. The large, marble-topped reception desk was set back a good distance from the main doors and Joseph trudged up to a hatchet-faced woman of about fifty who sat behind it. She remained completely unmoved by his presence, engrossed in one of those sex-and-shopping tomes set in Hollywood. Only when Joseph cleared his throat did she deign to put her book down, look up and offer him her undivided attention. 'Yes?' She managed to make the single word convey both distrust and impatience.

Joseph explained that he would like to speak to Tina Ferreira's supervisor and the woman immediately set her face in a scowl. Questions followed: did he have an appointment? No. Was he a police officer? Not exactly. Not exactly? Joseph lied and explained his role was more on the investigative side, as an assistant to the public defender. That did not go down well, either. Did he have identification? Nothing official. She closed her book with a finality that made Joseph realise he would not be going anywhere, then gave him a lecture on the excessive amount of time Tina's boss had been forced to spend in the past few days assisting the police and fielding reporters' questions. Joseph opened his mouth to speak but she concluded their conversation with, 'Unless you have a warrant or a better reason than that then I can't let you through. Good day.'

Of course Joseph could have argued with her further, and quarrelled himself into a police cell for claiming to be someone he was not. Instead he decided to cut his losses with a 'thank you for your time, miss', the last word accurate enough to cut her to the quick. Joseph left her to her Hollywood fantasy world.

As Joseph trudged away, a white-haired maintenance man in grey overalls walked passed him carrying a mop and bucket. With his free hand, the old man struggled to wrench open the fire-exit door to one side of the lifts. As he reached the main door, Joseph checked and glanced back towards the woman on reception. She'd gone back to

146

her book and wasn't paying him any attention so he decided to risk it. He walked over and pulled the fire door open for the old guy, who mumbled something so incoherent it might have been a thank you or a fuck you, as he passed through.

Joseph followed the man and they emerged in a gloomy stairwell. It was a bare little alcove, far removed from the brightly lit reception. The walls and metal staircase seemed to go on spiralling eternally upwards in an unbroken splash of battleship-grey paint. There was a long-forgotten table on the ground floor with one of its legs missing and the dull-brown door of a store cupboard in front of them but the rest was an expanse of grey wall. The maintenance man was already clanking his metal bucket up the staircase when Joseph called after him. He adopted the direct approach.

'Say, you interested in making a hundred bucks?'

The old guy stopped in mid stride then slowly turned back to face Joseph. He eyed him suspiciously and frowned. 'Not if it involves sucking your Johnson I ain't.'

Joseph winced at the suggestion. 'That isn't what I had in mind, believe me.'

'Keep talking.'

'I just need to get access to one of the floors here.'

The old man put down his mop and

bucket and folded his arms. 'Now why in hell would you need to do that, unless you up to no good?'

Joseph had hoped money would talk and explanations might not be necessary but the maintenance guy was in no hurry to let that happen. 'I'm a journalist and I'm doing a feature on that girl who got herself killed the other day. I just want to have a look around, see where she worked, what her desk looked like, if she had photographs on it or maybe a pot plant, what view she had from her office window, that kind of thing. We call that flavour.'

'Flavour, huh?' the old guy seemed doubtful that this could be worth a hundred dollars.

Joseph pressed on. 'But the lady on the front desk won't let me go up there.'

'Lady? Annie ain't no lady, she's just a dried-up, mean old cunt that hates the world. Who you with anyhow? The *Times?*'

Joseph shook his head. 'I'm not that lucky. It's one of those websites, you know the kind of thing.'

'Yeah,' said the old guy, who clearly did not. 'But I could still get fired.'

Then why are you still talking to me, thought Joseph, unless you are just trying to get the price up. He was keen to take a look round the building but only as far as TJ's one-hundred dollars would take him. He took the dirty money from his wallet. It had been burning a hole in there ever since the dealer gave it to him. 'Well, like I said, I got one-hundred dollars here, which is good pay for a short loan of your overalls.'

The old guy's eyes narrowed greedily when he saw the note and he scratched his chin thoughtfully. 'I guess I could take my break early,' he said craftily. 'Go for a coffee across the street.' He started to unbutton his overalls and pull them down over his shirt and jeans. 'If I was to leave these here overalls lying on that table there and someone was to take 'em when my back was turned...'

'Exactly,' said Joseph. 'Thank you.'

The old guy shrugged. 'You got the greenback.' He snatched the bill from Joseph's hand, before adding, 'That young girl used to work on the eighth floor, turn right when you come out of the door and walk down almost to the end. Her desk's on the left, as far as I know they ain't changed nothing yet, what with her body still being warm and everything. Won't take 'em long though. There's a striplight out not too far from her desk and there's a box of bulbs in that storeroom, along with a stepladder. The door's open, don't take nothing else.'

'I won't, thanks.'

'I'm just trying to make sure you don't get lost or stopped by security. If you do get caught you ain't seen or heard of me ever, you hear.'

'I guarantee it.'

'You better or I'll kick your ass for sure.'

'They likely to notice a new face round here?'

'Doubt it,' muttered the old guy. 'I've worked here seventeen years and not one of them even knows my name, miserable sons-of-bitches.' And with that he was gone.

Joseph donned the overalls which didn't fit him all that well, being too short in the leg and too tight round the chest. He prayed no-one would notice. It was never like this in the movies, thought Joseph, when some secret agent knocks out a guard and steals his clothes they were always a perfect fit, but this was real life and things were rarely that neat and tidy. He found the box of strip lightbulbs and took out two just in case one happened to be a dud. Despite the old man's warning he picked up a couple of screwdrivers as well then he tucked the stepladder under his arm and took the stairs slowly, meeting no one on his long ascent to the eighth floor. By the time he reached his destination he was sweating and breathless. That old guy must have been fitter than he looked.

When his breath returned, he opened the door into a brightly lit office, peopled by workers with their heads down, all of them tapping away at their own PCs or taking phone calls quietly. No one paid him any attention as he walked along their corridor. There was little talk aside from low voices on telephones and certainly no banter of laughter. No one was busting anyone else's chops as Eddie used to say. It was as if the building's sense of humour had been surgically removed, the kind of place where everyone was just a wage slave, keen to get to the end of their day with the minimum of fuss and get home again.

Joseph noticed everybody had a blue name sign on top of their PC so he kept his eyes peeled for Tina's. The offending light was the only one in the corridor missing a bulb so Joseph halted and brought the ladder out from under his arm. As he swung it round he upended a metal wastebasket and a guy in a brown suit looked up irritably from his phone call. 'What the hell?' he said.

'Sorry,' said Joseph and he pointed to the offending light. 'I could come back later?' as if it really didn't mean anything to him either way.

'No, no,' said a greasy-haired middle-manager who emerged from a tiny, glass-walled office, trying to look as if the troubles of the world were on his broad but capable shoulders. 'That bulb's been in the book for weeks. What kept you so long?'

Joseph shrugged and did a good job at looking simple. 'Busy, I guess.'

'Well, you're here now,' said the manager curtly, before adding, 'Are you the new girl?' which puzzled Joseph until he realised a young woman was standing nervously behind him waiting to be assigned a desk. Before she could answer the manager said, 'Come with me,' and he walked back into his glass cubicle with the newcomer. I bet he loves that damn office, thought Joseph. Brown suit had already gone back to his phone conversation so Joseph unfolded the stepladder right beneath the bare light and climbed up to it. From that height he could easily pick out the name on a PC at the only empty desk nearby – it was Tina Ferreira's.

Joseph took out a screwdriver and slowly unscrewed the plastic cover, all the while looking at Tina's desk. It was just like all of the others except for the usual few personal touches they were allowed. There was a picture of Tina with an older lady who could have been her mother. The unfortunate woman was probably back in Cuba right now, nursing a broken heart for her poor dead baby. There were no further clues to the mystery here though – just a battered cuddly toy that sat on top of her computer, a souvenir from home maybe, and a metal penholder with a couple of cheap biros. In amongst them were a yellow highlighter pen and a pencil with a novelty rubber character on the end. It had long, wobbly arms that would wave manically every time you moved it. It gave Joseph an inexplicable feeling of sadness to think this was all that remained of Tina Ferreira here.

He removed the plastic cover from the light and was rewarded with a puff of dust in his eyes and a small shower of crisp insects cascading onto his shoulders. They had crawled in and died there months ago and been slowly done to a turn over time beneath the heat of the bulb. Joseph brushed the bugs from his overalls and climbed down holding the cover, which still contained a number of perfectly preserved insects stuck to the plastic. He turned to a plain young girl with a sympathetic face and said, 'Mind if I stack this against your desk a moment?'

'No, sure, go for it,' she said with a needy smile. The girl's name was Sarah, according to her blue sign, and she seemed startled to be spoken to at all. Joseph needed someone like her right now; shy and eager to be liked. 'I didn't realise where I was until just now,' he said, shaking his head. She listened but clearly didn't understand his meaning. 'That poor girl,' he added and she immediately cottoned on.

'Tina, yes, it's terrible.'

'Worse for you,' he said sympathetically,

'being close colleagues and all. Were you two friends?' Joseph surmised she didn't have many in this office.

'I guess,' she said doubtfully. 'She was nice and a hard worker, saving for college, you know.' She lowered her voice conspiratorially. 'I mean not everybody is from "over there", if you get me – a hard worker I mean.'

Joseph nodded like he got her. He was about to continue when the manager emerged from his office with the new girl and asked, 'What are you doing?'

'Just passing the time of day while I get the bugs out of this here light.'

'Well don't, she's got work to do.'

'He was just asking about Tina.' The girl meant this in Joseph's defence but he wished she hadn't said it.

'What about her?' asked the manager, immediately going on the defensive.

'I was just saying what a terrible thing to happen to such a nice, hard-working young girl,' said Joseph.

'Really?' said the manager without hiding the look of irritation on his face. 'Well maybe you've been watching too many news bulletins, if we'd known what she was mixed up in, frankly we'd never have hired her.'

'What kind of things?' asked Joseph but the manager immediately clammed up.

'Never you mind,' he said 'Are you going

to fix my light, or what?'

'Sure,' said Joseph, 'but I got to go get my other screwdriver first. They got little itty bitty screws inside where the bulb comes out.' Joseph gambled that this lie would go undetected since it was unlikely the manager had ever peered inside one of these lights himself.

'Jesus,' muttered the manager impatiently and he marched back into his office. The new girl wandered away to an empty desk.

As soon as his back was turned, Joseph caught Sarah's eye and mouthed the word "what?" at her. She lowered her head and whispered, 'Seeing guys.' Then she added, 'Lots of 'em,' like she had never heard of such an outlandish thing.

Joseph gave a low whistle as if it really was a strange old world out there but Sarah was too nervous to carry on talking to him in front of her manager. 'Excuse me,' she said it like she needed to pee and walked away. As soon as her back was turned, Joseph walked right up to Tina's workstation for a closer look. He had no idea what he was likely to find but it was then he noticed that she had some other photos pinned to the partition behind her computer. What he saw stopped him in his tracks. One of the snaps was a picture of three young girls drinking cocktails with little green umbrellas in them. Mugging for the camera was Tina

Ferreira and with her were two other girls acting like they were her best buddies. One of them he couldn't place, but the second was none other than Maritza, and they were all drinking together in the Meteor. Joseph looked round again to make sure he was unobserved, then he tugged at the photo and it came away from the board along with its drawing pin. He stuffed it into the pocket of his overalls and walked away leaving the bare light, its wires exposed and a plastic cover full of baked insects propped up against Sarah's desk. Joseph went straight through the door to the stairwell. When the door closed behind him he broke into a run.

10

So that was what old Samuel meant when he said it was Tina's job that got her killed. He wasn't talking about the admin she was doing for CDS Xenon, he meant her dangerous little sideline. Tina Ferreira was moonlighting as a hooker and Maritza was running her for TJ. The young, tax-paying, hard-working girl, darling of the evening news bulletins, hung out with dope peddlers in her spare time and turned tricks for TJ for extra cash. Bet she wasn't declaring that income to the revenue, thought Joseph grimly as he drove away from the building.

Joseph's cell phone trilled shrilly and he glanced at it. The number was not one he recognised and he answered it cautiously.

'Hello.'

TJ's deep, unmistakeable voice asked him, 'Are you ready?'

'Yes.'

'Meet Ray in Harlem in one hour, club called the Nightspot behind Lenox Avenue, got it?'

'Yes.' Before he could add anything the line went dead. There was certainly no chance the FBI would ever pick up anything useful monitoring TJ's calls.

As Joseph headed towards Harlem, he thought some more about Tina Ferreira. Her moonlighting had to be the reason someone killed the young girl. He had now established a definite link between the murder victim and TJ and Baxter. Cyrus's refusal to work for Baxter explained why he had been set up as the fall guy for her killing. Of course Joseph still did not know why TJ and Baxter wanted Tina dead, if all she was doing was sleeping with their clients for money? What did she know? What had she seen that was so important they couldn't let it go? He supposed in her line of work it could have been anything. Joseph knew he was not even halfway to resolving this one and he was still well short of the proof needed to spring Cyrus from jail. All he had so far was an insight into the secret world Tina Ferreira inhabited while her colleagues were home with their families, tucked up in their beds at night. It was a world most normal law-abiding people would never see or come close to, but Joseph was going to have go deeper and deeper inside it if he was going to discover the truth.

Poor little Tina, the immigrant girl who dreamed of a bright, new future in America, had got herself in way too deep and, as Joseph edged his cab towards Harlem, he had to wonder if he was any different to the young girl from Cuba. Had he bitten off way more than he could safely chew?

It wasn't hard to find the Nightspot, a big, sprawling club that occupied a converted warehouse in Harlem. Joseph asked to see Ray and he was shown into a back office that Baxter seemed to treat as his own, even though the club was presumably owned by TJ. Baxter was perched behind a large desk covered in phones, a computer and the usual bank of CCTV screens that blinked at them from one corner. It was virtually the only light in the room, for the window was blocked by thick, wooden shutters. Joseph realised Baxter lived with the constant threat of assassination from rival gangs, so his life had to be a closed, shuttered world of blocked windows, cars with bulletproof, privacy glass and a phalanx of bodyguards that followed him everywhere. Joseph wondered what it must be like never to be able to go for a walk, buy your own newspaper or ride solo on the subway. Was the money and power really worth all that?

Baxter surveyed Joseph as if he was something he'd just picked up on his shoe. Then he muttered, 'You on time at least.' He nodded over at a burly black man in a plain grey suit seated on a couch. A ludicrously chunky, solid-gold watch sat on his wrist and a single thick gold chain hung round his neck over a black polo neck shirt. He sat bolt upright on a sofa too small for his bulk, looking like he had been waiting for Joseph to show up so he could leave. On his lap was a black, leather overnight bag that he clasped tightly to him as if it contained his only possessions. 'This is Mr Marley, not his real name of course but you can call him that if you have to call him anything at all. Meanwhile he knows who you are, so bear that in mind if you're tempted to screw up today. Take him where he wants to go. Now get out of here both of you, I got shit I need to be doing.'

The silent Mr Marley rose from his seat, followed Joseph out of the club and climbed into the back of his cab. Joseph got behind the wheel and waited for his instructions. When none came he risked a glance into the rear view mirror and asked, 'Where to?'

The big man seemed to wake from his trance then. He muttered an address before resuming his silence all the way back to the Bronx. Joseph wondered if Mr Marley had been given his fake name after the world's most famous reggae star. If so, perhaps Baxter had the merest glimmer of a sense of humour beneath his cold exterior.

The next few hours followed a rigid pattern. Joseph would be given a street name and would head straight there. As soon he reached it, Mr Marley would give an instruction on exactly where to pull over. He would reach into his case at the last moment and take out a large block of product wrapped in tin foil that had been painted black to make it appear less obvious. Then he would climb from the cab, being careful never to leave his bag in there with Joseph. Mr Marley would then walk into run-down premises that were a front for the drugs trade; a low-grade peep show, crumbling bar or clip joint, or sometimes just a vacant, boarded-up lot that had been turned into a temporary drug den. Occasionally a man would simply emerge like a wraith from the shadows, having waited patiently in the cold for an expected delivery. On these occasions, Joseph would actually witness the transaction, as a block of pure-tar heroin was palmed quickly to the dealer, who would scuttle away with the merchandise under his jacket. No money changed hands here but TJ's reputation and the violent tendencies of Baxter were probably all that was needed to ensure the agreed payment followed each week at a pre-arranged time. Woe betide anyone who tried to skim off the top from TJ's operation, thought Joseph.

The system was almost perfect, as a taxi cab was unlikely to arouse the suspicion of the police in the same way that a car would if it was seen zigzagging across the Bronx all afternoon. Even so, Joseph felt his heart beat faster whenever a black-and-white drove by. On one occasion, a police car behind them suddenly turned on its flashing lights then emitted a piercing whoo-whoo from its sirens and Joseph's heart sank, but the car quickly overtook them on their way to another call.

Joseph knew what he was doing was indefensible in the eyes of the law. It seemed a very long time since he had first lectured Cyrus on the folly of working for gangsters. He had even called Cyrus a drug dealer and now he was doing exactly the same thing as his friend, though he told himself that this was different. Joseph wasn't in it for the money. He knew he had to somehow gain the trust of Baxter and TJ, if he was to have any chance of bringing them down and saving Cyrus, and the only way to do that was to shepherd this man around.

After a half dozen drops, Mr Marley announced he was leaving, but Joseph should continue ferrying a Mr Hendrix wherever he wished to go. He gave Joseph five-hundred dollars before the new dealer joined him. He was black, just like all of the guys who had melted into view from the cold, dark shadows, a fact that depressed Joseph more than he could say. Did young black males in the Bronx really feel they had no other choices? It broke his heart to think about his own son growing up in a world like this.

Joseph did another four trips for Mr Hendrix, a man who was as economical with his words as his predecessor. He spent the afternoon driving down streets he would have gone nowhere near in his normal shift, but with the protection of TJ hanging over his dealer, like some evil halo, they were safe.

It was depressing work. As he waited for a transaction to be completed, cadaverous figures emerged from street corners to congregate round their dealer as if they could smell the arrival of a new consignment and wanted to be first in line for a fix. Skeletal boys, still in their teens, and young girls, whose lives were over before they had even started, since they were already one rung down the ladder from the whores who sold themselves on street corners, shuffled into view. They would be hoping the meagre hauls from their petty crimes would be sufficient currency to purchase some of TJ's golden product. Joseph wondered how anybody could be so dead in his soul to make money out of this much human misery. Wherever TJ and Baxter resided these days it was already a hell of sorts.

Eventually, he was given another five-hundred dollars by Mr Hendrix and told to fuck off. Abruptly, Joseph's first afternoon's work as a drug courier was over. Easy money, he had been told. Well he had been paid a thousand dollars but there was nothing easy about it.

Joseph took a couple more fares in the early evening but his heart wasn't in it. He'd been shaken by what he had seen outside the crack dens and heroin houses of the Bronx. To think this could happen in a place like America, the richest country in the world. It made him even more determined to bring down Baxter and TJ.

Joseph's last fare that day was a run out to the airport. He picked up ninety bucks from a couple of business types who were stressing out about that month's lower-than-expected sales figures. Joseph wanted to tell them he envied them their troubles. With some honest money in his pocket finally, he decided to clock off early and head home to Yomi. At this rate he might even be able to prepare something edible for dinner beforehand.

The traffic kept moving and Joseph found himself driving just a few blocks from the Meteor. Maritza would probably be there and he still had a whole bunch of unanswered questions. He was early so what harm could it do to swing by there?

When Joseph walked into the Meteor, he saw Baxter standing at the bar with another man. He couldn't see the second guy's face as his back was turned but the brown leather jacket was unmistakeable. Here he was again, the driver of the cab that had been shot up when Tina died. This time Joseph felt he understood his role in the whole affair. He was now convinced that the driver, far from being the innocent victim of a shake-down by drugs dealers looking to intimidate an innocent man, was one of TJ's most trusted men. Either that or he just liked to spend all of his money and most of his waking hours hanging out at the Meteor with gangsters, which seemed unlikely.

Maritza was behind the bar and she eyed Joseph as he approached the group. Baxter didn't look exactly pleased to see him but some of his earlier illwill seemed to have worn off.

'Joseph, Mr Marley told me you was cool today. He said you kept your mouth shut and did what you was told. Maybe you're learning the way we do things round here.' Before Baxter could continue, his mobile phone rang and he fished it out of his pocket. When be realised who it was, he left the group, calling an introduction back to Joseph as he went. 'This here's Esi Kobena, he's a friend of ours.' He said it like they were all in the mafia together. He thinks he's Donnie Brasco, thought Joseph. 'Maritza, pour them both a drink,' ordered Baxter as he walked out of the room, talking quietly into his phone as he went.

Joseph introduced himself to Esi Kobena. 'Nice jacket,' he said when he was sure Baxter was gone. 'I think I saw it on the evening news.'

'Oh, you did, did you?' Kobena was sheepish. 'Yeah, well I didn't want no publicity, not with a killer on the loose out there, who could still be looking for me and all.'

Kobena didn't look too nervous to Joseph. In fact he was a portrait of calm, considering he was meant to be the sole witness to a brutal homicide. 'That's funny,' said Joseph. 'I thought they got the guy that did it.'

There was a brief flash of panic in Kobena's eyes but he recovered quickly.

'Maybe they did, but the cops don't want me talking about it. I ain't s'posed to confirm or deny anything, you understand.'

'I understand.' Joseph thanked Maritza for his whisky and took a sip. He normally made a point never to drink anything alcoholic until Yomi was in bed; that was too easy a habit to get into but he had been shaken by what he'd seen today and he felt as if he needed this one. 'It must have been a heck of a thing to be caught up in though.'

'It was. To tell you the truth, I thought my time was up. "This is it old Esi" I told myself but you know what?'

'What?'

'God must have been on my side that day, that's what it was, and Jesus and all his angels, the way those bullets went through the glass and missed me. It could only have been one of God's own miracles, yes, sir. He was guiding my hand as I turned that wheel.'

'Guess so,' said Joseph, though he wasn't buying any of that Bible-belt bullshit for an instant. Esi Kobena certainly didn't look like a trailer-trash evangelist even if he sounded like one. 'Shame he wasn't on the side of that poor young girl, too.'

'Well now, maybe she's just in a better place, you never know, you just have to have faith.'

'Amen to that,' said Joseph piously.

'I felt bad for her, real bad you know, her dying like that and everything, but I'll tell you the truth, brother, if it's got to be her or me I'd much rather it were she, you know what I'm saying.'

'I think so,' said Joseph. 'So where were you taking her that day?'

'Why'd you ask?'

Joseph shrugged. 'Just making conversation.'

'Uptown,' said Kobena with a finality that left Joseph under no illusions. 'Anyway, I got to be going now.' He drained his drink hastily. 'See you around. You be cool now, you hear.'

Joseph wondered if Esi Kobena even knew how to open his mouth without a lie coming out. With him gone, Joseph was left alone at the bar with Maritza. This time she wore a tight, red shirt buttoned up the middle but only far enough to show her figure to its full advantage. Joseph had to admit she was distracting to look at and damn if she didn't still remind him of Apara.

Maritza spoke first. 'So you're working for TJ now, huh? You think that's a good idea?'

'You tell me, you work for him, too.'

'It ain't the same. What I do here is legal.'

'I'm not talking about serving drinks.' Maritza quickly looked away. 'No, you do a different kind of work, too,' he said quietly. 'And so did Tina.'

Maritza looked scared. 'How'd you...' and she stopped herself from completing the sentence.

'I hear things.'

'Well, you shouldn't hear things. It's dangerous to hear things. Baxter'll cut your motherfucking ears off if you hear things, don't think that he won't. I've seen him do worse. Don't you know how crazy he can get? You don't want to be crossing him, nor TJ. Not if you want to keep breathing.'

'So they keep telling me.'

'Well, it's true.' She said it with feeling. 'You should listen to them, Joseph. You seem like a nice guy, so why do you want to get mixed up in all this? You should get away from here, while you still can.'

'Tina was one of your girls, wasn't she?'

'What do you care? You a cop?'

'You know I'm not a cop. You know where I'm from and how long I been over here. You know just by looking at me that I'm just like you. Except I ain't scared, not like you're scared. I can see it in those big, beautiful eyes of yours. You're terrified, Maritza. But what you got to be so scared of? I thought TJ looked out for you 'cos you're his brother's girl.'

Maritza gave a bitter laugh. 'I'm AJ's girl alright, 'cept I ain't seen him in three damn years. They put him away for five and he won't let me come visit. Says it's too hard to see a woman when you can't be with her. So now I got to wait for him and I ain't got nobody.'

'How does TJ treat you? He look after you?'

'Oh sure, I'm a well-treated prisoner. I get to eat, drink, even do a bit of blow from time to time. I'm just not allowed to go anywhere or see anyone.'

'Tina was going some place. Heard she was saving for college. Is that why they got mad at her? What exactly happened to Tina?'

'She was shot,' sneered Maritza. 'Didn't you see it on the evening news?'

'And why did they shoot her?'

'What's Tina to you?' she asked suspiciously. 'Did you even know her?'

No, but I've known a hundred like her, he almost said. 'A friend of mine cares very deeply about what happened to her. He just needs to hear the truth, Maritza.'

'There ain't no truth, 'cept what you heard on the TV. Someone took a potshot at Esi and hit Tina in the head, poor fucking bitch.'

'And Esi just happens to work for Baxter who works for TJ, while Tina worked for you and you work for Baxter and TJ. I ain't a cop but I found that out pretty quickly. How long do you think it'll be before the cops work it out, too?'

169

'Why should I care?'

'You tell me, Maritza, you're the frightened one.'

'I ain't scared?' she snapped, banging her hand against the counter top in frustration. 'Now leave me alone!' And she turned sharply away from him just as Baxter came back into the bar. He noticed the girl's hostility and gave them both a look. Joseph feared he had gone too far, questioning Maritza so obviously on Baxter's home ground.

Baxter approached him and looked Joseph directly in the eye. 'I think you are right, Joseph, Maritza doesn't like you. I wonder why. I can see anger in her eyes. Get me a drink, Maritza.' The girl walked away to obey him and when she was gone, he ordered Joseph, 'Tell me what you just said to her.'

Joseph stared back into Baxter's merciless gaze then he picked up his drink and swallowed a mouthful. He said, 'I told her what no woman ever likes to hear.'

'Go on.'

'That she'll never be happy.'

'Why not?'

'Because to be happy, you have to know what you want and I never met a woman yet that knew what she wanted.'

Baxter took a moment to digest this then, finally, he laughed. Maritza returned with his drink and he told her, 'Joseph understands you bitches better than I thought.' She looked hurt but dared not contradict him. 'It's time you were going, Joseph, walk to the door.' Baxter meant for Joseph to follow him for a private word. As they walked, Baxter said, 'TJ is going to use you again soon. He trusts you after that stunt you pulled with the grease-ball's gunman, but me, I don't trust anyone, least of all some guy who walks straight in off the street asking me for a job. We're not stupid men, Joseph, just 'cos we ain't been to no college or nothing. Fools don't build empires. Do you think I am a fool, Joseph?'

'Of course not.'

'Good, because if you do take me for a fool I swear I will make your little Yomi an orphan before his next birthday, then I'll cut his face up so bad he'll never forgive his old man for the looks you left him. You got a handsome young boy. Make sure he stays that way.'

This time Joseph did not wait for Eddie's arrival before his drink. Instead, he poured himself a large glass of whisky and sat down in his old armchair looking out of the window as the sun began to set over the projects. Yomi would be home soon and he'd be concerned to witness his father drinking but Joseph would tell his son he had a toothache. He wasn't entirely sure the boy would believe him but he badly needed a drink.

Baxter was right; he had underestimated the man. He'd been stupid enough to believe he could hang around drug dealers without involving Yomi but they had checked him out and now they knew about his young son. Joseph had thought he could move in and out of the world of Baxter and TJ without affecting his life at home. He had made that mistake before when he was stupid enough to take the word of his superiors in Lagos. They had told him they wanted to clean up the force, investigate their own officers and root out the insidious evil of corruption that had stained the reputation of the NPF, and he had believed them. Then, when he finally got close to the men at the top, the puppet masters who pulled all the strings, the men with the money who did what they wanted and bought their own justice, he had found out the real truth. They had come to his house in the middle of the night, poured petrol through his front door and set light to it. Only the man they sent botched the job. Joseph was away that night, chasing down a lead in Abuja, when his home had gone up in flames with his wife still in it. If Yomi had not been staying with his grandparents that night he would have been taken from Joseph, too. When Joseph finally discovered that Oba Matusa had been paid to burn down his home, the puppet masters were still one step ahead of him. Oba had been shot up on the highway before Joseph could get a name out of him.

When the newly widowed policeman still showed no signs of halting his investigation, the word had gone out on the streets. There was a big contract on the life of Detective Joseph Soyinka. So he was forced to run. Joseph took his son and the little money he had and he ran, all the way to America. Now it seemed he had learned nothing from Apara's death. Joseph cursed his stupidity but there was no going back. He was in far too deep for that.

Joseph heard the key turn in the lock and Yomi's soft footfalls padded up behind him. There was no greeting from his son, who merely walked off towards his room.

'Yomi,' called Joseph, 'come here.'

The sound of the footsteps on the barely carpeted floorboards ceased and resumed again as Yomi turned and reluctantly walked towards his father. Joseph had not turned to face his son, so, when Yomi walked around the chair and was framed by the window, the sight Joseph took in shocked him. The boy had one eye almost completely closed from the effects of a heavy blow. His cheek was swollen and puffy and the skin around the eye was discoloured with bruising. For a moment Joseph thought Yomi had been roughed up by one of Baxter's men to ensure his father fulfilled his side of the bargain until Yomi looked at his father and said flatly, 'it wasn't my fault.'

'You've been fighting again?' asked Joseph incredulously.

'Yes.'

'Despite everything I said to you.'

'It's not that easy,' said Yomi defiantly, as if his father had no idea about the real world. Joseph could not believe he would have to speak to his son once again on the subject of violence. It was the last thing he needed right now.

'I told you before that I would drop it once, Yomi, but now you've broken my trust and I want to know who you've been fighting and why.'

'I can't tell you.'

'You are going to tell me,' he insisted.

'No, I'm not.' Then Yomi shocked Joseph by running off to his room and slamming the door behind him.

Joseph was stunned his gentle young son was acting this way and his first thought as he leapt from his seat was to kick open the door and re-establish his parental authority. There would be some harsh words and accompanying punishments. Something made him think again, however, and instead he reached for his mobile phone.

Brigitte DeMoyne had said to call if he ever needed to discuss Yomi and this seemed like a good time to take her up on the offer. Perhaps a woman might have a different perspective on the matter and she was the one teacher Yomi seemed genuinely fond of.

She answered on the third ring. 'Brigitte, it's Joseph Soyinka, I'm sorry to bother you.'

'That's okay, Joseph,' she said brightly and, despite all the troubles he had right now, he was immediately struck by how nice her voice sounded on the line. 'I'm glad to hear from you. I said you could contact me any time.' There was a moment's hesitation as Joseph tried to find the right words so she prompted him, 'What can I do for you?'

'It's Yomi,' he began.

'Oh, of course,' she said and for a second it sounded to him as if she thought he had called for another reason.

'He came home with a black eye and bruises all over his face. To tell you the truth I'm starting to worry about him getting into fights. Have you noticed anything strange going on lately?'

There was a silence on the end of the line that went on so long Joseph wondered if he had been cut off. 'Hello?' he said finally.

Brigitte sighed. 'So, you didn't get my letter?'

'What letter?'

Brigitte explained that she had written to

Joseph because Yomi had started a fight at school. Again Joseph was shocked. He thought he knew his son and yet it seemed he did not. How could this gentle boy get himself involved in so many fights in such a short period of time? Now it seemed he was even starting them. And what had become of the mysterious letter? There could surely only be one explanation. Joseph wound the conversation down with Brigitte, thanking her for taking the time and trouble to write to him and assuring her he would take the matter very seriously when he talked it through with his son.

'That's okay, Joseph, it was nice to hear from you,' she said before she quickly added, 'I mean it's nice that you care so much for your son, not all of the parents I see are like that. He's a good kid, maybe he's just going through a bad patch.'

'Maybe, well he will just have to come through it and I mean right now.'

'Okay, well, I can see you have things to discuss with Yomi and I hope you don't think I'm interfering but it might be an idea not to be too hard on the kid. This isn't like him.'

'Thank you for your time, Brigitte,' said Joseph and he immediately regretted the way it sounded. To his ears his words were abrupt and dismissive, as if he wanted the lady to mind her own business. Straightaway he wanted to correct himself. He should tell Brigitte how much he appreciated her help with Yomi but it was too late.

'Okay, Joseph, no problem,' she said quickly, as if she had detected the same tone from him. 'Goodbye.' Then she hung up before he could return the farewell.

'Damn it,' he said aloud when she had gone. Brigitte DeMoyne was about his only female contact – other than a wise-cracking, middle-aged neighbour and the girlfriend of a drug lord – and now he had ruined that. Could he do nothing right these days?

There was no time to ponder his latest error. Joseph put down the phone and walked into Yomi's room.

Yomi was finally sleeping when Joseph pulled on his coat and went out into the freezing-cold corridor. It was unlikely his son would wake during the night, particularly after the draining conversation they had battled through, but Joseph had left him a note just in case. He was on a job, it said, with no more detail than that.

The late-night call from Baxter had been unexpected but it was almost a relief to be out of the apartment. The cold air nipped at the flesh on his face as he went to collect the cab. It was going to be a hard winter this year.

As Joseph drove to the Meteor for Baxter's first pick-up, he went over the argument with Yomi. As soon as he had burst into his son's room, Joseph accused Yomi of stealing the letter from Brigitte DeMoyne. Mercifully, Yomi did not even bother to lie about it and Joseph was able to just about contain his temper while he heard his son out. Yomi turned out to be a tougher nut to crack than some of the suspects Joseph had questioned back in Lagos. Whatever he was hiding from his father he fully intended to keep it a secret, but Joseph kept on at him, determined to uncover the truth. In the end Yomi gave in, too exhausted to resist the ceaseless questioning. What he told Joseph shocked his father to the core. Yomi claimed he had been fighting because he had been asked to take drugs by some other boys in his class and refused.

'What kind of drugs?' asked Joseph, stunned that an eleven-year-old boy could get access to drugs at all. 'Marijuana?'

'Not just weed, no,' said Yomi, and Joseph wondered how his son could have suddenly aged ten years right there in front of him, not only calling the drug by a street name but seemingly dismissing it as one of the milder options available to him.

'What then?'

'Ice,' answered Yomi.

'Ice?'

'You know, Crystal Meth.'

'Oh my god, you were offered Crystal

Meth?' Joseph could not believe it at first, but his son's face showed him this was no game of make-believe. 'Yomi, I want you tell me the truth, did you take any?'

'Of course not!' snapped Yomi. 'That's why I ended up like this. I told them no, just like you always say to.'

'Did you report it to anyone, your teacher?'

'Do you think I'm an idiot? No, I didn't want to get into any more trouble, but it made no difference.'

'Why?'

'Because the drugs were found in their lockers, my friends got expelled and they think I ratted them out.'

'But you didn't.'

'No.'

'And they did this to you?'

'Yeah, some, so I fought back. I don't know what you want me to do.'

'You said these guys are your friends.' Joseph shook his head. 'Yomi, they aren't your friends. Friends don't do drugs and beat each other up.'

'What do you know about it? You're not an American.' And Joseph couldn't think of any words to counter that argument. Instead he took a deep breath and regarded his son, who was lying on a pillow, his baseball mitt within easy reach and pictures of his favourite players cut out of magazines and pinned to the walls. Yomi was still a child but one of his eyes was closed up completely and his entire face was puffy with bruises from punches administered by his so-called friends.

Yomi had resisted peer pressure which was one of the hardest things to do when you're a boy. It's hard enough when you're a man, thought Joseph and his mind went back to Lagos and all the approaches in locker rooms, coffee shops and parking lots. "Take the money, Joseph, turn a blind eye, Joseph, do the sensible thing, Joseph". That's what they used to tell him when they tried to pass the brown envelopes full of cash. When he refused, it was always the threats that came next; to his career, health and family, and they were unceasing.

More than anyone, Joseph knew how hard it was to withstand peer pressure and the heavy price you had to pay sometimes to be your own man.

'You should have told me before.' Joseph moved towards the boy. Yomi flinched but his father pulled him close and hugged him. 'I don't like you fighting, Yomi, but you didn't take the drugs.' Joseph wrapped his arms tightly round his son. 'I'm proud of you because you didn't take the drugs.'

By the time Joseph pulled up outside the Meteor a fine rain had coated the building with a sheen of water making it an even less welcoming sight than usual. His instructions were to remain in the car and wait. Presumably his arrival would be picked up instantly on one of the CCTV cameras and his latest-charge would emerge from the Meteor carrying a bag of fresh drugs for distribution. Who would it be this time? Mr Marley, Mr Hendrix, or another shadowy figure from Baxter's gang of dealers? Joseph received his answer soon enough. A door at the side of the club creaked open and out stepped a gaunt, wiry figure wrapped in a dark raincoat, hunched against the rain. Even from a distance, the menacing figure of Baxter was unmistakeable.

He climbed into Joseph's cab and said, 'Pleased to see me, huh? Yeah, you look it.'

Joseph was tired of Baxter's permanently threatening air. Maybe it was losing impact from its endless repetition. 'No, just surprised. Didn't think you'd be getting your hands dirty down here in the streets like this.'

'I'm from the streets and now and again I have to get back out there,' Baxter sneered. 'Thought I'd take you with me, Joseph, so I can keep a good, close eye on you. You see, you and me are on a special job tonight.'

'Yeah?'

'Oh yeah.' Then he laughed. 'You could say we're going over to the dark side.'

11

Baxter was talkative on the journey, which meant he was either high or drunk. Whatever he had been taking, he was about as pleased with himself as it was possible to be.

'TJ ain't the only one with brains round here, Joseph, you remember that. He might be the boss, for now, but he's been at war with those greaseballs for three years and he ain't won yet.'

'What's he doing wrong?' asked Joseph as mildly as he could under the circumstances.

'Nothing,' snapped Baxter. 'He just needs to be doing a little bit more that's right. All this time killing each other and where has it got us? We need to be talking to our enemies.' He laughed. 'That's what we are going to do, Joseph, we are going to talk to our enemies. You see they need us. The greaseballs been having a hard time lately, on account of how someone clipped Pinto, their second-in-command.' He sniggered at the memory. 'They used to say he was one tough motherfucker. How tough is he now, huh? Anyways, product has become a lot harder to come by since the man with all the contacts was offed and that stimulates demand. Tonight we going to meet that demand.'

'You're saying we are going to sell drugs to the Puerto Ricans. Are you serious?'

'There's greaseballs and greaseballs, some of 'em get all riled up and send gunmen to the Meteor and they are going to regret doing it, believe me. Others are more realistic, they got the greenback and money talks. Hey, they don't care. They'll get their product from anyone who's got it. Black, white or yellow it don't matter to them and it don't matter to me, as long as the money is green.'

'Does TJ know about this?'

Baxter took his gun out and tapped it against the window behind Joseph's ear. 'Listen, motherfucker, you let me worry about what TJ knows and doesn't know, you hear.'

'I was only saying...'

'Well, don't say shit.'

'I thought you wanted to beat the Puerto Ricans, not make then stronger.'

'All in good time, Joseph.' He laughed a high-pitched stoner laugh. 'All in good time.'

Sure enough, Joseph was directed to a new corner of the South Bronx that none of Baxter's men had visited before, presumably because it was controlled by the Puerto

Ricans. He pulled up outside a derelict warehouse and waited as Baxter emerged from the cab with an exaggerated nonchalance. It had to be incredibly dangerous for Baxter just to be in this neighbourhood when he was right-hand man to TJ, the Puerto Ricans' most dangerous enemy. Whatever truce he had negotiated to do this deal was liable to be a flimsy one and drug dealers weren't known for their sense of honour. No wonder Baxter was high tonight.

Baxter must have read his mind for he leaned into the driver's window and said, 'You better hope I come back. They won't want no witnesses.' And he laughed again at the thought of Joseph being gunned down and buried alongside him.

Joseph spent a long ten minutes waiting in his cab and eventually Baxter returned looking relieved and satisfied. 'Let's not outstay our welcome,' he told Joseph, who was happy to get going.

As they were moving away, Baxter slid five hundred dollar bills through the slot at Joseph. 'Take it,' he said. 'Or I'll start wondering what you are doing this for if it ain't the money.'

'There ain't no other reason,' said Joseph firmly, then he folded the notes and stuffed them into his shirt pocket.

Baxter was looking at the rest of his money

and grinning. 'A good night's work.'

'I still don't get it,' said Joseph. 'But maybe that's why I'm just a cab driver.'

'You don't, do you?' said Baxter. 'Put it this way, aside from the money I just made, which don't mean shit to me incidentally, we just gave those fucks some product that's going to make them very popular with their regular users. It's real special. I call it cocaine on the rocks and it's going to drive the greaseballs off our streets for good.'

Baxter wanted to go straight back to the Meteor and Joseph was pleased to be rid of him. Baxter was bad enough when he wasn't high, with drugs inside him there was no knowing what he might do.

As soon as Baxter left him, Joseph swung by the rehab clinic. There was a young man dressed in a white lab coat on duty at the front desk. At first he didn't notice Joseph as he was so intent on his paperwork.

'Do you have a box for donations?' asked Joseph.

'Er, yeah, sure, screwed to the wall over there.' He eyed Joseph curiously. 'They empty it every evening.' The young man meant there was no point trying to rip it off the wall.

Joseph ignored the implication that he was a criminal. He walked up to the far wall, withdrew the five crisp one-hundred dollar bills from his shirt pocket and stuffed them into the locked metal box.

The following morning Joseph went to visit Cyrus at the County Jail. Two prison guards led his friend into the room and steered him to a seat behind a toughened glass barrier. The only communication permitted here was by phone. They must really think Cyrus is a category 'A' hardened gangster, thought Joseph. It was laughable. It seemed ridiculous to be talking to a man on a phone when his face was just inches from yours, so close in fact that the physical signs of the strain Cyrus was under could be easily made out. Joseph's friend looked terrible. The flesh under his eyes was sunken as if he had barely slept since his arrest.

'Hello, Cyrus, how's it been? Bad?'

'How do you think?' Cyrus was fighting back the tears now. Seeing his friend from the outside world threatened to bring all of his emotions bubbling to the surface. He sniffed back the tears and composed himself, and his tone lightened. 'Thanks for coming to see me. You're the only one, 'cept my landlord.'

'Your landlord?'

'Yeah, Mr Orovsky came to see me. He actually came here. I thought he was visiting me and what a nice guy and all, but no. He came all the way out here to tell me he's going to kick my stuff out if I stay in here, because I have no way to pay the man his rent. He says I got a week to get his money.' Cyrus shrugged and snorted. 'A week. I'm stuck in here to be charged with murder and this fool says I have a week.' Cyrus shook his head. 'It's a nightmare in here, Joseph. Yesterday a big mean guy I've never seen before walks straight up to me in the exercise yard. He tells me if I say anything about Baxter to the police or my lawyer I'll get shanked. Do you know what that means, Joseph?'

'Yes.'

'They have these homemade knives they make out of bits of metal with tape wrapped round the handle and they call them Shanks.'

'I know.'

'I've got four sisters and a brother back home. I send them money. If they don't get the money, my little sister and brother they don't get to go to school. They all relying on me and they don't even know I'm in here. What are they going to do if the cops put me away for this murder. I'll be an old man before they let me out. Sometimes in America they send people to prison for life with "no prospect of parole". That means you die in prison. I'm in court again in two days. What happens to my family if they do that to me? You know the shame they'll feel if their brother's in prison? Won't matter to all the folk they know back home whether I'm innocent or not. I'll be in an American prison so I must be guilty of something.'

All the while Cyrus was talking, Joseph tried to think of something, anything he could say that would bring him some fleeting comfort, some crumb of hope to puncture his despair, but what could he say? How could Joseph explain, on a prison phone line that was far from secure, that he was in the process of infiltrating a gang of heavy-duty drug dealers to try and solve Tina Ferreira's murder all on his own? It would sound fanciful, it sounded ridiculous right now even to Joseph as he ran it through his mind.

'Cyrus, it will be okay, I promise. Leave the landlord to me, give me his address and I'll speak to him.'

'What are you going to say? Don't give him any of your money, Joseph, please. Don't do that.' The idea of Joseph's charity seemed to bring on even more agitation in Cyrus. He was literally wringing his hands as he pleaded.

'I said I'd speak to him and I promise I won't give him any of my money,' he said. 'Leave it to me, okay.'

'Okay,' said his friend wearily.

Joseph took down the address and chose his next words carefully in case someone was listening. 'Now I'm still asking around about the shooting and so is Eddie. If we hear anything, anything at all, we'll get straight onto that hot-shot lawyer of yours and give him the news, alright.'

This flimsy assurance seemed to brighten Cyrus for some reason. 'Yeah, great, man, thanks.'

'In the meantime I got a more recent picture of the girl that was killed. She looks different here and I was wondering if you knew her or had ever seen her before?' Joseph had taken the photo of Tina and her friends out of his pocket and pressed it up against the glass for Cyrus to squint at. 'She's the one on the left.'

'No,' said Cyrus. 'First I saw of her was when the cops spoke to everybody at the Impala.'

'So you never saw her, never picked her up, bumped into her at the Impala or the Meteor?'

'No.'

'You sure?'

'Yes,' said Cyrus, 'but...' He seemed confused.

'But what?'

'It's just ... I know the other girl, the one in the middle.'

'You know Maritza?' asked Joseph in surprise.

'Don't know her, no,' he said perplexed for a moment. 'That's not what I mean.'

'What do you mean then?'

'I've seen her.'

'When?'

'She was my last fare that night before I came to meet you at the Impala. I picked her up outside the Meteor after I seen Ray.'

'Are you certain, Cyrus? Absolutely certain?'

'Of course. I'd remember her alright, she's a good-looking lady. Wore the shortest damn skirt I've ever seen.' And Cyrus managed a half-smile at the memory.

I bet she did, thought Joseph, to make sure you were looking up it while she was sliding a gun down beneath your car seat. So Maritza planted the murder weapon that killed her good friend Tina on poor, unknowing Cyrus. She would have to have been real scared of somebody to agree to that.

As soon as Joseph left the prison he went to see Cyrus's landlord, an old, hard-faced Russian guy who lived in Mott Haven. The old guy answered the knock on his apartment door by opening it as far as the length of its chain and peering suspiciously out through the gap. 'Vot you vont?' he asked sharply, as if Joseph was a debt collector or the law.

He explained he was representing Cyrus, as the man could hardly attend himself, and he wanted to make an arrangement regarding the rent. Joseph was reluctantly admitted and allowed to sit at the tiny table in a dingily lit kitchenette. He was not offered a drink, nor would he have accepted one, as the place was filthy. Whatever past Mr Orovsky had, these days he obviously lived alone. Joseph's intention was to reason with the landlord but he very quickly realised that wasn't going to work and his well-rehearsed catalogue of Cyrus's woes was abandoned, its opening salvo falling on stony ground.

They were rebuffed in fact with the words, 'How old you think I am?'

Joseph was nonplussed. 'I have no idea,' he lied. The guy had to be at least seventy five.

'Eighty,' he said, before asking, 'You know ven I left Russia?'

'How could I?' answered Joseph, already tiring of the game.

'1945. Know what happened in 1945?'

'The war ended,' answered Joseph, feeling incredibly tired again all of a sudden.

The old Russian nodded. 'Ze vor ended,' he agreed. 'Know how many Russians died in zat vor?'

'No, a hell of a lot I should think.'

'Twenty million.' He curled his hand into a fist at his side, as if it had happened just yesterday and it was all Joseph's fault. 'Twenty million,' he repeated, wild eyed. 'I see this with my own eye and you come to

191

me and say my friend he has problem,' Mr Orovsky sneered. 'Ve all have problem.'

Joseph sighed. 'How about I just pay you the next month's rent?' He reached into his wallet and took out some of the cash he had been paid for ferrying TJ's dealers around. It wasn't as if he would be spending it on anything else and there was a certain irony in Ray Baxter paying Cyrus's rent for him, so Joseph felt he could justify bending the rules this time.

'Okay,' said the Russian simply and he held out his hand.

Eddie lifted his knight between two arthritic fingers, frowned at the board then set it back down again. He took a sip of his whisky and a long moment to reflect before finally moving a pawn forwards.

'I made a couple of calls today, Joseph, friends of mine who are still on the job, asked them a few questions.'

'Oh yeah?'

'I started with Alphonse Jakes. He's still in Bayside for what it's worth, but prison records show he's had a visitor, one repeat visitor in fact. Do you know who that could be?'

'I think I can guess.'

'One Theo Jakes, none other than his little brother, which got me to wondering if he ever answered to TJ.'

'I'm willing to bet he just might.'

'I wondered if my mind was going when I couldn't remember him at all, but it turns out Theo Jakes is as clean as a virgin's conscience. This guy not only has no rap sheet, there's no previous of any kind, no known aliases, not even a mention in a police file. Shit, he don't even have a driver's licence.'

'I think his brother brought him over from the Islands to take over the operation as soon as Alphonse knew he was going away.'

'I think so, too,' said Eddie. 'That's how it works. Before they're sent down, they hand over a going concern like this one to someone they absolutely trust. Trouble is, being drug-dealing, murdering, lowlife motherfuckers they don't know too many people of a trustworthy disposition.'

'So they keep it in the family,' agreed Joseph.

'Blood being thicker than water.'

'It's all starting to come together now,' said Joseph before sending his bishop on a long diagonal trek across the board to capture Eddie's neglected knight.

'Oh, Jesus,' muttered Eddie. 'I didn't see that coming.'

'You got another one.' Joseph nodded towards Eddie's second knight.

'You realise, if chess had been invented in America,' groaned Eddie, 'the horse would be the most valuable piece on the board.' Then he sipped his whisky reflectively, before adding, 'Of course we playing in New York, where they got more queens than horses.'

'Assistant Chief McCavity would get you suspended for talking like that.'

'Give me a break, Joseph; I got nothing against queens, just like I got nothing against spics, spooks, kikes, wetbacks, goombars or greaseballs. I'm not prejudiced, my friend, you know that. I hate everyone.'

The next day, TJ summoned Joseph to the Meteor. He still hadn't quite gained Baxter's trust but it seemed that since the night of the attempt on his life, TJ had seen something in Joseph that he liked.

'There's a bunch of Ginnys across the Hudson waiting on a delivery,' explained TJ. 'It ain't drugs but I don't want you looking inside the envelope, you hear. And I don't want my usual crew knowing anything about this, you got it? You got to go there now and they are a sharp crew. They'll know if you opened it.'

Joseph shrugged. 'What I don't know can't hurt me.'

TJ handed over an A4-sized padded bag and Joseph took it. 'Address is on the envelope,' said TJ, 'but not the name. You are taking it to a guy they call Mikey Junior. All these Ginnys name their kids after themselves, so everybody gets called fucking Junior. Mikey Junior'll probably still be Mikey Junior when he's eighty fucking five. Make sure you tell his crew the package is from TJ and it goes to Mikey Junior only. And I got a message I want you to give this big shot.'

On his way over the Hudson River, Joseph wondered how he had suddenly become a messenger boy for the New Jersey Mafia. Eddie had told him endless tales about the bloodthirsty Italian crews who had operated on his old patch so he knew all about Mikey Junior. He may have had a name like a Mousketeer but this guy was feared and respected on both sides of the river, having been credited with taking his father Mikey Patroni Senior's family into a new era. Eddie explained how twenty-first century ideas like people trafficking, ID fraud, credit-card cloning and hard-core subscription movies on the Internet featuring rape and torture had been combined with the traditional methods of the previous century; like prostitution, loan sharking, protection rackets and the diverting of union pension funds along with a little armed robbery just for fun. And then of course there were the drugs.

Joseph parked his cab outside a dingy-looking trattoria called Parmenteris. The place was closed. In fact it looked so dark and unappealing it seemed almost designed to turn people away, a useful front and no doubt a handy money laundering operation rolled into one. He was met at the door by a young soldier from the Patroni family who patted him down then brought him through the restaurant to a back room where he finally met the boss.

Mikey Junior had to be two hundred and fifty pounds, most of it stomach. Maybe that's what happens when they make pasta in your headquarters, thought Joseph. He was dressed in a loose, short-sleeved shirt that hung out over his trousers but failed to disguise the bulk beneath it.

'This is from TJ,' Joseph said, and one of Mikey Junior's lieutenants took the package from him and handed it over to the boss. 'And I got a message.'

'Let's hear it,' Mikey Junior's voice was gravelly like that of a one-hundred-a-day smoker. His pudgy hand tore open the package like it was made out of tissue paper.

'He says everything is there, all the details, what's missing is the names.' Joseph hoped Mikey Junior would understand this enigmatic message for he himself could not expand on it.

The boss was now looking at a red, hard-backed notebook he had pulled from the envelope. It was the kind people use to keep their accounts. He opened it and flicked through some of the pages. 'Anything else?'

'He says you'll get all the names when he gets the money.' Then Joseph braced himself for he had heard about Mikey Junior's legendary and fiercesome temper. The boss glanced up momentarily at Joseph, perhaps gauging whether he was being disrespected or not.

'Take this guy outside,' he growled and the young soldier seized Joseph by an arm and steered him towards the door. Then the boss said, 'Tony.' The young man stopped in his tracks to await instructions. 'I'll be a while, get him a beer...'

The soldier took Joseph out to a table in the corner of the restaurant then brought him a cold bottle of Peroni. He handed it over resentfully, like it was a waste of his talents to be doing this when he could be out killing someone for the boss instead. Joseph decided it would be a wise move to thank him and drink the beer down. Just as he was draining the last mouthful, Mikey Junior's lieutenant came out of the back office and told him, 'Tell TJ it's on.'

12

When Joseph gave Mikey Junior's short message to TJ back at the Meteor the gangster seemed pleased. 'Since I can trust you to do what I tell you without handling the goods, I got one last little job for you before you finish,' he smirked. 'You can take Maritza home.'

Maritza was waiting outside in the doorway and she climbed wordlessly into his cab. Despite the cold, she wore no coat. Instead she was dressed in hooker uniform of short skirt and black stockings with a teasing gap of flesh between them, and a low-cut T-shirt that showed half of the goods on offer. Joseph was amazed she didn't feel the cold but then wondered if she had taken some blow.

Maritza didn't speak at all on the way home except to give him her address. He watched her in his rear-view mirror and, when she turned slightly, the yellow glow of a passing streetlamp caught her in its glare and Joseph understood why she was keeping quiet. The side of her face was swollen and discoloured with bruising. Suddenly she started, her head shooting round to stare at a car that passed them coming the other way, as if she half expected it to turn and follow them.

'What is it?' Joseph asked but, as the car moved away, she immediately calmed.

'Nothing, just one of them big old BMW X5s. Ray drives a black one just like that.' Her voice sounded unconvincing when she added, 'Thought he might need me for something.'

The only thing Baxter might need her for was another beating, thought Joseph. 'Ray been slapping you around?' he asked gently.

She laughed. 'No, Ray don't slap me round. I'm AJ's girl remember? Besides, Ray dreams of laying a hand on me but not like that. This ain't what you think. It ain't nothing.'

'Isn't it? Looks like something to me.'

'Well it ain't,' she spoke firmly. 'And it wasn't Ray.'

'So, who then?'

Maritza took a long while to answer him. 'TJ,' she said finally. 'He's just tense on account of how he has this big deal coming up.'

'And you stepped in his way? Trod on his toes maybe?'

'Something like that.'

'So TJ beats up his big brother's girlfriend, that's nice.'

'I had it coming. You wouldn't understand.'

'Maybe I wouldn't.'

But Joseph *did* understand. Whoring was just another thing that was the same the world over. You started them out young, found them when they were straight off the bus or, in Maritza's case, the plane, running away from a past they didn't want to think about. Then you pretended to be their friend, bought them some cheap stuff, took them out for a burger maybe and, for some of them, this would be the first act of kindness they'd ever received. Then you made it clear that, if they loved you, sex with them was expected and that was probably okay too. After that you'd twist that deal a little further until it became, 'If you love me you'd have sex with this guy I know.' Pretty soon there'd be other guys and before they knew it they were in deep, taking the drugs you kindly provided them to remove the pain and the dead feelings inside them at the end of every working day. Get them addicted, take all their money, maybe just lock them away each night. That's how you got a girl like Maritza started. Sometimes, if you were lucky, even months later when you no longer ever touched them except to beat them up, they still loved you, because they didn't know any better. Maybe with Maritza it was a little different. At some point AJ must have decided to keep her all to himself, so he got her to stop the whoring and run the other girls. Still, Joseph was sure it was how he'd got her started. That story was always the same.

Maritza lived in a fifth-floor walk-up in Morris Heights and as he was dropping her off, Joseph said, 'Take my number, in case you need to call.'

'Why would I need to do that?'

'You never know,' said Joseph reasonably. 'Why not take it anyway. If you don't need it then don't use it. It ain't costing you anything.'

Maritza shrugged, took out her mobile phone and keyed in the number Joseph gave her. Then she said, 'You want mine?'

'Why not?'

She gave a cynical little smile. 'Yeah, why not?'

Maritza told him the number and he stored it under the name Debbie, in case TJ and Baxter ever felt the need to scrutinise his contacts. He wondered what name she had stored his number under – asshole probably. As Joseph put his phone back in his pocket he realised he only had numbers for three women in there. One was Marjorie, the other Brigitte and now there was Maritza; an old lady, a school teacher and a madam, he thought ruefully.

Maritza climbed slowly out of the cab and it looked like she planned to be gone without a word, then at the last moment she turned back and said, 'You can come up for a drink, if you like.' She said it like she was doing him a favour and it didn't really matter to her either way. She had already started to climb the big, brick steps to her front door as he made up his mind. Joseph followed her, receiving a teasing view all the way up her long legs as Maritza led the way in front of him. He should have blushed and looked away but the way she walked in that loose-hipped manner made him realise it was deliberate and he was pretty sure she knew the effect she was having on him. Even with that bruise on her face and the life she'd been leading Maritza was still a beautiful young girl. Joseph always found himself torn in her company. Mostly he wanted to look after her, though he wasn't sure quite why, but some of the time it was hard to ignore the obvious attraction between them. He told himself he wasn't her brother or her friend and he couldn't fight everybody's battles. You are doing this for Cyrus, he reminded himself. One problem at a time, Joseph, he thought, as they climbed the stairs.

The building was a low-rent, dark and foreboding place and Joseph could see why she might want some company. Perhaps that's what the drugs were for; to quell all the fear in Maritza's life. There seemed plenty of it.

When they finally reached her door, Maritza fumbled in her bag for the key and he realised her hands were shaking. It was no surprise when she dropped it on the mat and Joseph bent to retrieve it. He opened the door and led her inside, his hand on the cold bare flesh of her arm. She was freezing.

The flat was tiny and bare, containing nothing remotely personal; no pictures or plants, no books or newspapers, no reminders of home. The furniture looked rented and the apartment could have belonged to anyone. Maritza lived in a vacuum of work and sleep. There wasn't a thing in here you wouldn't mind turning your back on in an instant.

'Why don't you sit down and I'll make us a drink?' he asked.

'How about a whisky?' Exhausted, she let herself drop onto the sofa then kicked her shoes off and lifted her feet until she was curled up on it.

'How about coffee?' he asked.

'Why not both?'

Joseph nodded and went into the kitchen, found the whisky bottle and some tumblers, made the coffee and brought it all back in on a bare wooden tray, which he set down on the floor, as she did not have a table. Joseph sat on the other end of the couch at Maritza's feet.

'You said I wouldn't understand about TJ and you, so tell me.'

She laughed grimly. 'You got all night?'

'I ain't in a hurry.'

Maritza thought for a while. 'He ain't all bad, despite what I say. Sure he can fly off the handle but he protects us girls.'

'He protects working girls?'

She seemed reluctant to admit it at first but then she said defiantly, 'Yeah, me and some others I can't name.'

'Like these girls?' asked Joseph and he produced the photograph he'd taken from Tina's office.

'Where'd you get that?'

'It doesn't matter.'

Maritza sat up. 'You sure you're not some kind of cop?'

'No, but I have an interest in finding out the truth.'

She drew her knees up to her chest and wrapped her arms round them defensively. 'What kind of interest? You a private Dick? Who you working for, Joseph?'

'Just a cab company, Maritza, believe me. I'm no cop and I'm not about to let anyone bust you or hurt you. I just want to know what happened to Tina.'

'What's she to you?'

'Nothing, but a friend of mine is caught up in this. I'm just trying to help, that's all.'

Maritza looked guilty. 'You know that cab

driver they arrested?'

'You mean the one you planted the gun on?'

She looked away, staring at a blank wall. 'I ain't saying nothing 'bout that.'

'So, who is the girl in the picture with you and Tina?'

'That's Carolina.'

'Is she one of TJ's girls, too?'

Maritza nodded.

'Like Tina?'

The thought of Tina seemed to cause a great sadness in Maritza. The mention of her name caused her to slump down in the chair. 'Yes, Tina, too but I told you, she was trying to get out. She got a job, she stopped with the drugs.'

'But TJ wouldn't let her go.'

'No.'

'I still don't understand why he would kill her though, just for trying to get away. Give her a beating maybe, but murder?'

'Who says he...'

'Cut the crap, Maritza, we both know TJ had Tina killed. I can't prove it. I don't think I'll ever be able to prove it, but I would like to know what she did to end up with her brains blown out all over the back of a taxi.' The graphic image he painted was enough to shock Maritza into silence.

'Why did TJ kill Tina?' Maritza just stared back at him. 'Look, I'm not wearing a wire here, this is just between you and me and I know you want to tell it to someone. You've been dying to talk about it, only you can't because you're too scared. I can see it in your eyes. Maritza you've been scared for a long time, too long, but you don't ever have to be scared of me, so what happened?'

Maritza glanced down at her shoes and started to fiddle with the strap.

'You know I'm surprised you are under-estimating the cops like this.'

'What do you mean?'

'The things they can do now, not just fingerprints, there's DNA. If you left so much as a hair or a skin cell in that cab when you planted the gun, they'll know about it. Of course that's not enough on its own but if they get the idea you planted that gun then they'll be able to put two and two together. You probably weren't even wearing gloves, were you?'

'They got no reason to link me to that gun or that cab even.' Maritza was getting nervous and Joseph gave her a look. 'You ain't going to tell them?'

'That depends.'

She sat bolt upright. 'On what?'

'On whether you tell me the truth or not. You fill in the gaps I might be able to find a way to keep you out of this. If you don't, I'll just have to tell the police what I know and I guess the focus of their entire investigation will be on you. I don't suppose TJ will be too pleased when the NYPD comes crashing through his front door looking for you. Might be bad for business.'

'Oh god.'

'I don't want to do it, Maritza, I really don't. I want to help you but I got a friend looking at thirty years here. Doesn't that bother you? It sure as hell bothers me. Tell me what you know or I'll have to make that call.'

She took a long time to answer him and her words were faltering and unsure. 'TJ liked Tina at first. He liked her a lot. I guess she was kind of his favourite.'

'Then what happened?'

'She went with this new guy, didn't know who he was at the time but TJ found out and went crazy.'

'Who was the guy?'

'Nobody you'd know.'

'Come on, Maritza.'

'Pinto, Eduardo Pinto.'

'The right-hand man in the Puerto Rican gang?'

Maritza nodded.

'The same guy they found in a dumpster with a bullet in the back of his head?'

Maritza nodded again.

'But you say Tina didn't know who he was?'

'No, to her he was just a new trick, and

Pinto didn't know she worked for TJ neither, at least I don't think he did, but TJ thought she was passing information to Pinto instead of just fucking him now and again.'

'Information like when and where his drugs were coming in?'

'Yeah, TJ's been all wound up and crazy lately. It's a big risk for him whenever he gets a shipment. A half-dozen times a year he's 'fraid to death. He's trying to cut that risk by getting someone to put all the product he needs together and have it dropped in just once, but he knows if it goes wrong...' She didn't have to finish. TJ's plot was daring but very risky. The larger the drop, the more years the judge would add onto the sentence. Maritza added, 'He sees plots everywhere and says anyone who works for him is likely to turn traitor for money.'

'So that's why he killed Tina.'

Once more Maritza simply nodded.

'Then he took Pinto out, too, or did he leave that job for Ray?'

Maritza didn't say anything, she didn't have to.

'Does TJ still trust Ray, seeing as he doesn't trust anyone else?' asked Joseph.

'Trusts him, yeah, but he ain't happy with him, not lately, especially when the cops found Pinto's body so easily. TJ told him to make sure Pinto disappeared for good.'

'It seems like they say a lot of stuff to each other when you're around, Maritza.'

Maritza shrugged. 'I'm always there. They trust me and they know I'm not going anywhere.'

'Because they would kill you if you tried.' Once again Maritza did not want to acknowledge the truth of it to Joseph. 'There's just one thing you maybe haven't considered.'

'What's that?'

'You knowing so much makes you just about the most dangerous person in TJ's life right now, next to Baxter. You ever tell the cops what you know and he is looking at life behind bars.'

'He knows I'd never rat him out to the cops.'

'He thinks you won't, he hopes you won't but he don't know you won't. He can't be sure of that. We both know the sensible, safe thing a man in his position would do about a girl like you.'

'He wouldn't.'

'He killed Tina.'

'That's 'cos he thought she was...'

'He thought she was what? A traitor, a rat, his enemy all of a sudden? What's it gonna take for him to think of you like that? You smile at the wrong guy, talk to the wrong person, accidentally say hi to a bent cop and all of a sudden TJ hears. You said yourself he sees plots everywhere these days.'

'TJ owes me.'

'Why? Because you planted a gun on poor fucking Cyrus? That don't make him your friend. That's just another big fat reason for getting rid of you and you know it. Why'd you do it, Maritza? Why did you plant the gun?'

'They made me.'

'That all? You got nothing in return.'

'Once the shipment is in, they're going to let me go. That was the deal. I help them out and they help me get out.'

So it wasn't just fear of Baxter and TJ that made her plant the gun in the cab. They'd promised her a way out. Joseph wondered how long it would take Maritza to realise there was never a way out with a man like TJ.

'I'm going to sign up for a class, acting, in the evenings. TJ says he'll let me go.' She sounded desperate. 'You know who else came out of the South Bronx, Joseph? J-Lo? You know? Jennifer Lopez?'

Joseph nodded. 'Sure, I know J-Lo. I'm not from Mars.'

'I'm going to take this class, become an actress.' She was trying to convince herself it could happen. 'And I don't do the drugs like I used to either, but sometimes...' Maritza tried to stay optimistic but instead she began to cry and the words were almost lost in her breathless sobbing. '...it's hard to stop, you know what I mean?'

Joseph nodded and she slid into his arms, wrapping her own around his neck as her head pressed against his chest. He held her there tightly for a while as her body shook from sobbing. When she had finished crying she stayed there, pressed against his body and Joseph allowed it to happen. It seemed cruel to push her away. Finally she looked up at him and even though her face was streaked in tears he realised she was still beautiful. Somehow, she was still beautiful.

'I get so lonely. You the first person's held me in so long, Joseph.' Then she kissed him, quickly and suddenly. 'I can be kind, too.'

He could think of a dozen protestations, a hundred reasons why this was very wrong, but all he could actually say was, 'What about AJ?'

'I was with him for a year. Now I can't even remember what he looks like.' Then she leaned in and kissed him again before he could do anything about it. Despite himself, he couldn't help but relish the soft, hot touch of her lips and the warm breath of another human mingling with his own. God it would be so easy to kiss her back, to just let it happen. Her hand was on his chest now and she was pressing down with long slender fingers, her firm touch moving lower, down towards his belt and Joseph found that he could barely breathe. Maritza pulled the loose-necked T-shirt down with her free hand so he could see her bare, inviting breasts, and his senses were filled with the sweet musky scent from her body. 'I can be kind, too.' She whispered it this time, and there was something about the way she said it that stopped him short, it sounded like a pitch for business. Poor Maritza probably knew no other way to entice someone than by doing what she had always done, letting a guy touch her all over in return for a simple act of comfort.

'No, Maritza,' he said suddenly and he pushed her away.

Maritza looked hurt and rejected but, just as she had done in the bar, when he had declined her invitation to come home with her, she set her face hard and said in a voice made of stone, 'Jesus, what's wrong with you, you some kind of faggot or something?'

'No,' he replied simply.

'Well you sure as hell act like one. I ain't ever seen a man so 'fraid of a bit of titty.' She ignored the coffee, took a huge gulp of her whisky, drained the glass and climbed off the couch. 'I'm going to bed,' she said. 'You can let yourself out.'

13

They talked long into the night. Joseph knew he was close to unravelling the whole truth about the murder of Tina Ferreira but Eddie wasn't nearly so certain.

'I'm not sure what you've got, Joseph.'

'I've got a big-shot drug dealer who most likely murdered a bunch of taxi drivers three years ago because they wouldn't do what they were told. When he goes to jail he sends for his little brother, who takes over a lucrative operation specialising in drugs with a nice sideline in vice, just to keep the money coming in. The downside is he relocates to the South Bronx from New Jersey and starts a gang war with the Puerto Ricans.'

'So far I'm with you.'

'The murdered girl Tina Ferreira turned tricks for TJ but, unlucky for her, she wound up sleeping with Eduardo Pinto, right-hand man to the Puerto Rican's boss, on a regular, if purely professional, basis.'

'That piece of garbage,' said Eddie with feeling.

'I guess he was, judging by where the cops found him.' Joseph leaned forwards and poured the whisky, sharing the remnants of the Bushmills between their glasses. 'Sadly for Tina, TJ got paranoid and thought, probably wrongly, that she was passing information about his crew to Pinto.'

'Poor bitch,' said Eddie with feeling.

'So he killed her and then he got Ray to get rid of Pinto, permanently. Meanwhile our friend Cyrus...'

'He's your friend; I hardly know the sorry-ass motherfucker.'

'Do you kiss your daughters with that mouth?' admonished Joseph, before continuing, 'Meanwhile "our friend" Cyrus tries to leave the drug trade before he's barely begun his moonlighting as a courier and way before Baxter thinks he's earned the right.'

Eddie nodded sagely. 'No gold watch for Cyrus.'

'Which makes him the perfect fall guy for TJ. Either TJ or Baxter, it doesn't really matter who, since it was definitely TJ's idea, set up the hit on Tina, sending her off in a slow-moving taxi driven by one of their trusted drivers, Esi Kobena, the guy I met whose jacket you saw on the evening news. Now I'm willing to bet that if the police put a tail on that guy for a couple of days they'd be able to prove he is a courier for TJ.'

'Judging by the company he keeps and that smart jacket he wears.'

'I don't know what they told Tina. One last job for TJ and we'll let you go? Maybe, who'll ever know? Anyhow she gets in the taxi and off she goes but it's prearranged that Kobena will slow down on the corner and the hit man has plenty of time to step out in front of them and put a shot through the front windscreen that takes her full in the forehead. He walks away without a thought for finishing the driver, who is then portrayed as the intended victim of a gangland war, which suits everybody and has our friends from the NYPD swallowing the whole story. I'll bet Kobena told the police he'd refused to cooperate with the gangs and they were taking their revenge. Conveniently he gets a really good look at the hit man and, very bravely under the circumstances, fingers Cyrus, picking him out of an ID parade. Meanwhile the police search Cyrus's cab and straightaway they find the murder weapon. It all fits together so neatly for them.'

'It does if you care more about politics than solving crime, but that ain't police work. One of the first things this job teaches you is if it looks too good to be true it probably is. They were lucky with Mc-Cavity, too. Justice don't interest her, she just wants to tie up five murders in a hurry so she can look good in the papers and keep on rising.'

'Do you want to know the real beauty of TJ's scam. His brother's gun has been on ice for three years. Now he gets to use it to frame Cyrus for the cab murders, the killing of Eduardo Pinto and the accidental homicide of a poor young girl from Cuba. That's five killings perpetrated by at least three different people close to TJ and Cyrus gets the blame for them all. In the meantime Alphonse Jakes's name gets wiped from any link with a cold case on three unsolved shootings. I mean, it's beautiful really. If it wasn't so damned ugly I might even be impressed.'

'Trouble is, all you got to back you up is the word of AJ's coked-up girlfriend. You really think she's telling the truth?'

'Maritza's scared, Eddie, terrified I'd say. I think she has been itching to tell somebody the truth, it just so happened to be me.'

'But will she spill it to the cops?'

'Not yet, but one day she might wake up and realise the best thing TJ could do to insure himself against prison is to kill her. Then we'll see.'

'So what do you want to do about it?'

'I don't think I can wait that long. If TJ's big deal goes down before someone moves on him, he'll be unstoppable. Think of the finance behind him with all that new product he's going to spread around.'

'That's the thing. If this deal is as big as you say it is, you could lose him for ever. That's when they retreat into the big, gated compounds on the edge of the city, start acting respectable, then let someone else do the dirty work and take all the risk. You got to take a guy like that down while he's on the streets and still on the up. Otherwise you can forget about it.'

'That's what I figured.' Joseph gave his friend a significant look.

'What?' asked Eddie.

'I reckon now is the time to go to the police with everything I know but...'

'But what?'

'Are they really going to believe a humble immigrant cab driver from the South Bronx if he walks in there on his own?'

There was a long silence while Eddie contemplated Joseph's meaning. Finally he said, 'Not unless he goes in there with a highly respected former law enforcement officer from New Jersey's finest.'

'My thoughts exactly.' Then he leaned forwards and clinked his glass against Eddie's.

And so it was that Eddie made the call to the 41st precinct. Joseph was right to put his trust in the old man for, retired or not, the former police officer seemed to know just what to say to be taken seriously. Nevertheless, when he came off the phone, Eddie didn't seem entirely happy.

'McCavity won't see us, pressing engagements, which means she's blowing smoke up our ass but don't worry I wouldn't let it go. We have an appointment this afternoon with one of the guys working the case with her. A Detective Monroe.'

'That's great, Eddie. To be honest, he might take us more seriously than his boss.'

'Mmm,' murmured Eddie in agreement. 'So long as they don't fob us off with some wet-behind-the-ears-straight-out-of the academy type who only got his detective shield by blowing the commissioner.'

That afternoon, Joseph and Eddie set off for the precinct with Yomi in the back of the cab. Yomi's friend Freddie was having some kind of party at his parents' house and, since it was on the way, Joseph had agreed to drop off his son.

'Freddie's parents are going to be there, right?' asked Joseph.

'Of course,' answered Yomi.

'You make sure you're on your best behaviour while you're in their house.'

'Ye-es, Dad,' he chorused in that sing-song way kids employ when they are telling you they are not as stupid as you think.

'And make sure you thank Freddie's parents before you leave.'

'D'uh.'

Eddie laughed at Yomi's chiding tone. 'What's the occasion, sport?'

'What? D'you mean for the party?' asked Yomi.

'Yes, he means for the party,' said Joseph.

'Birthday,' answered Yomi quickly.

'Why didn't you tell me?' asked his father. 'You should have taken a present.'

'He only invited me yesterday, so I said I'd get him something later.'

'Only invited you yesterday? I thought you guys were supposed to be best buddies.'

'He wasn't sure it was going to happen. I guess he had to wait till his parents caved or something.'

'They are braver than me,' said Eddie. 'I'm used to punks and criminal lowlifes but I'd be too scared to throw a party in my home for a bunch of hoodlums like Yomi and his pals.'

'Thanks, Eddie,' said the boy.

'There gonna be girls at this party then, sport?' asked the old man.

'I guess.'

'Who you gonna try and kiss when they play spin the bottle then?'

'No one,' said Yomi sharply. 'I don't like girls.'

'Oh you say that now but give it a year or two,' smirked Eddie.

'He does like one girl,' said Joseph.

'No, I don't.'

'Now let's see if I can remember her name,' chuckled Joseph. 'Laura Williams, is it?'

'I don't, I don't.' Yomi was getting agitated.

Joseph could see through his rearview mirror that his son's face had flushed a bright red. Eddie was laughing, too, which only made it worse. 'Who told you that?' he whined.

'Just something I heard,' said Joseph.

'Yeah I heard it, too,' said Eddie. 'Think I picked it up on the police radio. They were saying "Yomi likes a girl, Yomi likes a girl".'

'No, I don't!' They both laughed. 'Shut up, both of you!'

Eddie stifled his laughter. 'Guess we heard wrong, Joseph. I suppose we'd better shut up about it, eh?'

'Maybe,' answered Joseph. 'I'll have to think about that.'

They travelled the rest of the way in silence and dropped Yomi at Freddie's house. They waved him off good-naturedly and waited till he reached the front door. As Freddie opened it to admit his friend, Eddie called through his opened window. 'Hey, Yomi, say hello to Laura Williams for me, yeah.'

Yomi went bright red again and the two men laughed as they drove away.

Joseph parked a couple of blocks from the 41st precinct and they walked the rest of the way. Eddie was never brisk on his feet these days but cold air and adrenalin seemed to propel him along. Eddie had polished his shoes until they were mirrors and he wore what he had previously described as his church-best suit.

Joseph held back for a moment to make sure there was no one around who could recognise him. When he was sure it was clear, they both crossed the street and walked into the 41st precinct.

At first Eddie thought his worst fears had been realised. The detective who was summoned to greet them at the front desk could have passed for a college senior. He was one of those detectives who preferred a dark suit and plain tie to a leather jacket. The suit was expensive-looking for a young man and the cuffs and collar of his shirt had been ironed into sharp creases, most likely not by him. Joseph guessed there was a wife or fiancée somewhere and she was happy to take a back seat, ironing the shirts and making sure there was food on the table for the young detective when he got home late. Monroe's type didn't court career girls. They didn't have the time or inclination. Monroe had old money and Ivy League written all over him.

'I'm Detective Aldon Monroe,' he said as he shook Eddie's hand. 'I'm pleased to meet you, Mr Filan and you must be Mr Soyinka,' he said before adding, 'the assistant chief asked me to meet with you today. If you would be good enough to follow me, I have an interview room lined up for us.'

Joseph was pleasantly surprised the young man took them seriously enough for such cordiality, but Eddie was less impressed.

'He even shaving yet?' he asked too loudly as they followed the detective along the corridor.

'Shhh,' hissed Joseph, who began to wonder if he had done the right thing in bringing Eddie.

Once they were seated in a windowless interview room, the young detective said, 'I understand you were on the job, sir?' He disarmed Eddie a little with his old-fashioned brand of manners.

'That's right, for almost forty years, on the other side of the Hudson.'

'Well Mr Filan, I know I don't have anything like your level of experience, but I'll do my best to get to the bottom of the problem.' He reached for a notepad and a fancy gold pen. 'Now, how can I help?'

Between them, Joseph and Eddie outlined the key points of their argument, including Joseph's conviction that Cyrus Agyeman was an innocent man wrongly held for murder. As Joseph described the drugs and vice operation run by TJ and Baxter, the as-yet-unofficial testimony of Maritza, who he did not name at this point, and the chain of events leading up to the death of Tina Ferreira, including the slaying of Eduardo Pinto, Detective Monroe diligently noted it all down in his book, the gold pen glinting as it darted from side to side like a metronome while he wrote. Sensibly, the detective did not interrupt with questions but allowed them to take him through everything Joseph had learned and, if his eyebrows momentarily shot up when Joseph admitted to his unofficial undercover operation, he did not pass comment on such an unorthodox approach to crime fighting. Nor did Joseph confide the exact nature of his work for TJ, saying only that he was employed as a driver, but Monroe did not have to be Columbo to work out what was going on. Again the young detective did not pass judgement. Instead he kept his own counsel.

Joseph knew he could easily be dismissed as a fantasist, but the presence of Eddie at his side gave more weight to his argument and he sensed ambition in Detective Aldon Monroe, which is why he saved the best part till last.

'TJ is waiting on a shipment. It's going to be big, larger than anything he has ever taken before and he's very nervous. I expect to be in on the drop. That's the kind of bust that makes careers, Detective Monroe, and I'm prepared to hand it to you on a plate, so long as you promise to undertake a close examination of the evidence against Cyrus.'

'Huh, what evidence?' said Monroe and

relief flooded through Joseph. The youngest officer on McCavity's team seemed to be the only one prepared to challenge her complete certainty that Cyrus was a professional hit man. 'But I admit I still have a number of questions.'

'We ain't in no hurry,' said Eddie.

'Good. Now I'd like you tell me more about this girl who works for TJ. What did you say her name was again?'

'I didn't,' replied Joseph, and the young detective gave a slight smile, as if it had been worth a try. 'She's no gangster. She's so terrified of TJ and Baxter she doesn't know what to do. I'd like to know what you could offer her in return for testifying against them both.'

'We wouldn't be looking to prosecute her, if that's what you mean. She's small potatoes compared to the men you've been describing. Of course I can't promise anything, but I'm sure something could be arranged to help her on the way to a new life. Now tell me again about this shipment...'

Joseph was in a buoyant mood when he finally left the precinct. For the first time since the case began he'd met a police officer who had not simply dismissed his reasoning as if he was deluded. Detective Aldon Monroe may still be young but he was most certainly ambitious, and surely this meant he was even keener to close the case and do it correctly.

Eddie's appraisal of the detective seemed to match his own. 'You can tell by the way that guy dresses he wants to get his ass up the ladder, which might just be good news for your buddy Cyrus. Some detectives I met think they are Serpico, they just want to smoke dope and dress like the perps they are trying to bust. He may be straight out of short trousers, but that boy can see there ain't no real case to answer except for a planted gun and a no-mark witness. I'd say we just did a very good day's work there, Joseph.'

'Let's hope so.' Just then, Joseph's cell phone rang. It was Yomi. There was a commotion in the background, sounds of panic and a lot of yelling. 'Yomi, what is it? I can't hear you.'

'Just get here, Dad, please.' Then Yomi hung up. Joseph knew his son would never behave like that without good reason, so he stepped on the gas.

'What's up?' asked Eddie.

'Don't know,' he said. 'But I don't like the sound of it.'

When they reached Freddie's home, they found the front door open. A young friend of Yomi's waved at them in a panic. They marched straight by him and up the staircase, passing two more scared-looking youngsters, who flinched back to let them by. There was no sign of any adults and Joseph finally realised why Yomi had been so evasive. This was an unsupervised party and now something had gone badly wrong. Joseph opened the first door he reached and found Yomi and Freddie with two other friends. They were standing over a young boy, who was lying on the floor by the bed.

'What happened?'

'We don't know. He's ill,' offered a youthful voice from somewhere behind him.

Joseph ignored it and stared down at the boy, who could not have been much older than Yomi. He was deathly pale and doubled up, holding onto his belly and groaning. White blobs of spittle clung to the side of his mouth and his eyes rolled. He started coughing and up came a thin thread of blood.

Joseph turned to his son, who was clearly petrified by the spectacle. 'Drugs?' His son just nodded. 'What's he taken, Yomi?' But Yomi was too shocked to answer. 'You?' Joseph demanded of the nearest boy, then he turned to Yomi's friend. 'Freddie, what's he taken?' Again he was met with silence.

Joseph realised they were all scared to death and nobody wanted to be the first to get into trouble, but they had a skewed sense of priorities. By the look of the boy on the floor he was in serious danger. Joseph shouted at the boys then. 'This is important! I have to know what your friend here has taken or he could die! Now, tell me before I start banging heads together.'

Yomi managed to blurt out the word, 'Blow,' and Joseph didn't know what was worse, to witness a twelve-year-old taking cocaine or to be told about it by his son, who just a year ago would have had no knowledge of such a thing.

'He's OD'd,' snapped Eddie. 'We got to get him to hospital.' He took out his cell phone and walked away to dial for an ambulance.

Joseph meanwhile was on his knees, cradling the boy's head while he thrashed around. 'Where'd he get this stuff?'

'Outside the school ground.'

'Where is it?'

One of the other boys brought a small bag that still contained a little of the white powder.

'Anybody else take this?' Joseph demanded and they all shook their heads.

'He was the only one,' said Yomi.

Joseph stuffed the bag into his pocket, then he gently lifted the boy in his arms and started to carry him down the stairs. The boy's head immediately went limp.

'He's out,' said Joseph. 'Where's that ambulance, Eddie?'

'On its way, but they gonna have a problem. Cross Bronx at this time of day?' Eddie was right, the rush hour had begun and a delay like that could cost the young boy his life.

'What's his name?' asked Joseph, as he took the boy out of the house and into the fresh air.

'Joey Neste,' said Yomi.

Joseph supported Joey's head while the boy's friends gathered round.

'Is he going to die?' asked one of them.

'We're going to get him to hospital and he'll be fine,' said Joseph, but Joey was already unconscious and it did not look good. Joseph turned to Eddie. 'I'm thinking I can get us where we need to be quicker than the ambulance. What do you think?'

'Hell at least we are here already. Let's not wait.'

'Come on then.' Joseph scooped up the boy and started to run towards the cab. 'Freddie, phone your parents and get them down here. Nobody leaves till then. Yomi, you come with me.' Then he lowered his voice, 'Eddie, phone the hospital again. Tell them we are going to take the kid to the drug rehab centre. It's close and they got docs there that'll know what to do.'

'Gotcha.'

Joseph drove along the side streets of the

South Bronx at a speed he had never come close to before. More than one pedestrian regretted stepping out into the road that day and was forced to dart back onto the pavement again. Passers-by must have thought someone had stolen the cab as it roared down side streets, took corners at a skid and bounced over bumps in the road. Eddie stayed in the back seat, cradling the unconscious child, holding him tightly to protect him from the worst of the bumpy ride. Yomi was in the front seat shocked into silence.

They screeched up to the front of the clinic. Joseph jumped out of the cab, took Joey out of his friend's arms then ran with him up to the front desk, with Eddie and Yomi following on behind. There, covering the afternoon shift, was Josephine, the nurse he had picked up days earlier. There was no time for reunions.

'I've got a young boy here. He's OD'd on coke!'

Josephine leapt out of her chair and ran round to the front of the counter. Others joined her and she barked instructions until they scurried away to prepare a room and the facilities needed to pump a young stomach clean of drugs.

'You sure this is just coke?' asked Josephine. 'It don't look like a normal OD to me. This boy look like he been poisoned.'

Joseph looked at Yomi imploringly, and his

229

son nodded furiously. 'Coke, yeah, from the Puerto Ricans outside my school.'

As soon as Yomi said it, Joseph realised the truth. This must have been coke from the batch Baxter sold to his rivals. What had he called it? Cocaine on the rocks. It was going to "drive the greaseballs off the streets for good". Contaminated cocaine. But what the hell was in it?

'If you know something, now is a good time to tell me,' said Josephine firmly.

'I think this batch is contaminated?'

'What with?'

The trouble was Joseph didn't know. Cocaine on the rocks? What did Baxter mean by that? Did Baxter mean ice and if he was talking about ice was he using the street name for another drug he'd thrown in there to poison the batch or was it just some joke name for another substance, like strychnine or rat poison?

'I'm not sure.'

'I'll take your best guess.'

'Crystal Meth? Maybe.'

'If you're right, we've got work to do.' As she spoke, a team of white-coated staff ran up to them with a gurney, lifted the boy onto it and whisked him away.

'Wait here,' Josephine called as she went after them.

They sat silently in an anteroom, waiting for

what seemed like hours for news of the boy's condition. Yomi couldn't look either of them in the eye. Eventually he said, 'I didn't take anything, Dad.'

'Not here,' said his father in a tone that brooked no contradiction. 'We'll talk about it later.'

Joseph was filled with rage and anger. He was annoyed at Yomi for telling lies and attending an unsupervised party where there were drugs readily available, but that was nothing compared to his anger at TJ and, most of all, Baxter. They didn't care a damn who died or got hurt in their war with the Puerto Ricans, just so long as they came out the victors. An Italian-American youngster like Joey Neste was just the latest in a long line of civilian casualties in an increasingly pointless and bloody struggle for the right to sell more poison to addicts. The only saving grace for Joseph was the fact that it wasn't Yomi lying there in a hospital room right now having his stomach pumped out.

Josephine reappeared after half an hour to enquire about the patient's background. Joseph explained about the unsupervised party and gave the boy's full name. Yomi was able to contribute the name of the street where he lived.

Josephine said, 'The doctors are doing all they can. I'm going to see if I can trace the

231

parents. I'll see what I can do.' Then she disappeared into an office to make some phone calls.

It was another hour before they saw the nurse again. She came padding down the corridor, the soles of her standard-issue white shoes making squeaking noises on the linoleum as she walked. 'Doc thinks he's got it all out. That boy is one lucky son of a bitch, if you'll excuse me. You might like to know that the doc said you working out what was wrong with him probably saved his life.'

'Thanks,' said Joseph. 'So will he be okay?'

'Hard to tell for sure, but it looks that way, as long as he don't get any worse in the next twelve hours. I finally got hold of his mum. She's on her way down here. Of course she's frantic, but she'll want to thank you.'

Joseph got to his feet. 'Tell her not to worry about that.'

'The police will be here, too. I had to tell them. It's not every day we get an OD this young, even here. So don't go anywhere. They're gonna want to speak with you.'

But Joseph was already pulling on his coat. Once again, the weariness had hit him. Days of not sleeping, combined with his worries about Yomi and the stress of trying to save Cyrus had taken their toll. Explaining everything to the detective then rushing Joey to St Mary's had finally tipped him over the edge of exhaustion. All he wanted to do now was lie down in a darkened room and make it all go away. He would speak with Yomi about all this but there was no hurry. His son was in shock and looked mightily chastened by his experience and that probably meant far more than anything Joseph could say to him just now.

'I got to get him home first. We both know the police won't be in a rush to take a statement from me about something like this, and they'll know where to find me.'

'How?' she asked.

'I'll leave you my cab licence.' And he handed the document to her.

Josephine must have seen the tiredness in his eyes and thought better about challenging him. Instead she just nodded and walked back behind the counter holding his licence.

Joseph took his son firmly by the hand and they left. Eddie walked slowly behind them, his joints having stiffened up from the long wait in a hard chair.

'Why are we in such a hurry?' asked Eddie as he reached the car.

'Get in, Yomi,' said Joseph and he waited till his son was in the cab and could no longer hear him. 'Eddie, I've been on the police radar ever since they picked up Cyrus. By now they must be starting to think I've got an intimate history with the drug trade.

I don't want them wondering if that over-dose had anything to do with me. Detective Monroe may have come round to our way of thinking, but he's the only one so far. You know how it is with this kind of thing. If I leave now they may not bother to come and see me at all. I'll drive back here and collect my licence tomorrow. Right now I just need to rest.'

It was then Joseph noticed the cab had a parking ticket on it.

Eddie had never really heard Joseph curse before but this time he went crazy. Before his friend could say a word, Joseph had torn the ticket out from beneath the windshield wiper and scrunched it into a ball. 'What did this fucker think I was doing parked outside a drug centre? Did the sorry asshole even so much as contemplate putting his stupid motherfucking face through that door to ask who owned this cab?' There then followed a further full minute of foul-mouthed and blasphemous curses from Joseph before Eddie could even attempt to interrupt the tirade and answer him.

'Joseph, calm down, you can appeal it.'

'Appeal it?' cried Joseph. 'I shouldn't have to appeal it. I should be allowed to hunt the no-account fuck down with a gun then make him shove his ticket up his own ass in a public place while the whole city watches and applauds!'

When they reached the project, Joseph said, 'As soon as we get home, you're going to bed, Yomi. No arguments.' His son did not answer and Joseph took this as compliance. Yomi had barely spoken five words since he'd seen his friend almost die from the doctored cocaine. A small part of Joseph wanted to reach out to his son, comfort him and tell him it was going to be alright but he knew this was one instance where he had to be cruel to be kind. Yomi had to learn the severe consequences of screwing around with drugs. Maybe something like this happening to him so young was what was needed to stop him ever messing with them himself. Joseph prayed the lesson had been learned.

Eddie left them on his floor and Joseph climbed the stairs with Yomi, fumbling for his key in the semi darkness of the corridor. They certainly didn't waste money on luxuries like safe lighting in stairwells here, which was a shame because nobody in this building ever trusted the lifts.

Joseph turned the key and reached around for the switch on the wall. Before he even turned on the light he knew something was wrong. The room felt different somehow and he could smell smoke. Joseph sensed the presence of another and, when the light came on and illuminated the room, his worst fears were realised. Joseph couldn't see anybody but his big swivel armchair had been facing the door when they left and now it was facing away from them towards the window. Cigarette smoke was rising from behind the chair in a long slow vertical trail. Someone was sitting there, had been for some time, waiting for them in the darkness.

14

With one hand, Joseph kept Yomi back in the corridor, for he was sure someone was about to kill him. At least the boy would have a slim chance of getting away if Joseph took the bullets.

'Who's there?' he called, fully expecting one of Baxter's men to rise from behind the chair, call him a rat and gun him down. Joseph cursed his luck. Somebody must have seen him walk into the 41st precinct that day after all.

But it was not one of Baxter's men. Instead it was the man himself who spun the chair round to face them. When the chair came to a halt, Baxter had a big, childish grin on his face liked he'd just finished a fairground ride. 'Nice chair, Joseph, bit old but the older they are the more comfortable the ride ain't that what they say? I've been here a while now. Where the fuck you been?'

'Working,' replied Joseph. He saw no point in trying to reprimand Baxter for his lack of respect in breaking into their home like this. Baxter presumably regarded Joseph as someone he owned. 'Then helping a friend move into his apartment.'

Baxter nodded. 'Well, you back now and we gotta get going. That your boy out there? Well bring him in. Let me take a look at him.'

Reluctantly, Joseph led Yomi into the room. From the look on his face Yomi had already worked out that this was not a good guy visiting his father. Baxter probably thought coming into somebody's house un-invited was quite normal but Yomi would view it very differently. Baxter smiled. 'He's a good-looking boy. Ain't you about to introduce me?'

'Yomi, this is Mr Baxter, a friend of your daddy's,' said Joseph.

Yomi couldn't fail to pick up on the tension in the room but Joseph was relieved when all he said was, 'Pleased to meet you, Mr Baxter,' and he held out a hand.

Baxter thought this was hilarious. 'Well lookee here, pleased to meet you too, boy!' He got up out of the chair and took the outstretched hand. He didn't seem to notice when Yomi flinched from his touch. 'Ain't he got the manners though, Joseph.' Baxter seemed impressed.

'You said something about going?' asked Joseph.

'Yeah, we got to go. Shipment's come in, everybody got to be there.'

'Now?'

'Yeah, Joseph now.' Baxter's tone changed and the menace instantly returned. 'You think we can just arrange this shit round your calendar?' Joseph frowned at him. 'Oh, do excuse my motherfucking language but I reckon he hears far worse in the playground, don't you? If he goes to school round here, he will, that is if he goes to school at all. Now hug him goodbye, Joseph. I want you with me tonight. So I know where you are.'

'Yomi, get your night things, you're staying with Marjorie tonight.' Once again Joseph was relieved to hear no argument from Yomi and Baxter chose not to contradict the plan. Joseph didn't want to leave Yomi on his own but right now he couldn't risk a meeting between Eddie and Baxter. Both men had keen instincts and would be instantly distrustful of the other and the ex cop was unlikely to survive the encounter. Marjorie was beyond suspicion in Baxter's world, but Joseph knew she'd never give up Yomi to anyone but his father and God help the man who tried to take the boy from her. Marjorie had a phone and Joseph knew she owned a gun, which was better than leaving his son alone in an apartment Baxter had already broken into with effortless ease. She was old but Marjorie was still quick-witted and about as hard as bullets.

Yomi looked scared as he sloped off to his room. He'd had one hell of a day for an eleven-year-old but Joseph knew it would get much worse if Baxter grew impatient. 'Be real quick about it, son. Daddy's got to go out with Mr Baxter now. Hurry up.'

Handing Yomi over to Marjorie had been relatively trouble free. Joseph apologised for the short notice but explained he had some work he really couldn't turn down.

Marjorie had been dismissive. 'Where in hell you think I was planning to go at my age, Joseph? It's colder than a witch's titty out there.' She glanced over at the sofa. 'Yomi's always welcome on my put-me-up, as long as he don't mind keeping an old lady company in front of the TV, eh boy?' Yomi gave her a weak smile and she must have detected his concern, for it was then that she finally noticed Baxter's malevolent presence lurking in the corridor. Joseph could tell she tried to hide her feelings, but it was clear Marjorie did not like the look of his new friend. 'Come inside now, hon,' she urged Yomi a little too eagerly. 'Don't let the cold air in with you.' Then she hustled him through the door then closed it behind her.

As Joseph walked away down the corridor with Baxter he heard bolts being drawn back from within.

It was one of those bitingly cold New York nights that keep people off the streets. The South Bronx was deathly quiet as they sped through it towards the docks. Joseph would have given a lot to be sitting in Marjorie's cosy little apartment right now in front of the electric fire with a glass of something warming in his hand. Instead he was forced to drive past empty pavements already turning white from a frost that couldn't wait till morning to put in an appearance. Baxter sat in the back, staring nervously out through the cab's windows, his head darting from left to right then behind, as he tried to work out whether they were being followed. He was agitated now that he was on the streets again. This is what it must be like to have so many enemies, thought Joseph.

'Keep your eye on that car back there, that red Jap number. He been following us for about four blocks.' As soon as Joseph identified the car, it darted away down a side street, its driver on an errand that had nothing to do with them.

Baxter leaned forwards in his seat. 'You had anybody come round asking 'bout me, Joseph?'

'Nope, can't say I have.'

'Of course you'd tell me if they did?'

'Of course.'

'Yeah, sure you would,' Baxter sneered, his anxiety putting him in an ugly mood.

Joseph chose every word carefully from then on and tried to make each one sound as unthreatening as possible. Baxter was in the wrong mood for any kind of quarrel. Joseph guessed he had reached the stage where he was using far too much of his own product, for he was beginning to display paranoid side effects. Imaginary people were following them in unmarked cars, others were visiting his associates, talking about him behind his back, plotting against him. Joseph had seen this kind of behaviour before from gangsters back in Lagos. It would be almost comical if it did not nearly always lead to people getting killed. He wondered for the thousandth time why anybody would take a drug that turned their friends into enemies. There was no car following them that night and Joseph had certainly never received house calls from any of Baxter's rivals. It was all in the man's mind. The irony was that Joseph could accurately be described as Baxter's enemy but not in the way he imagined, and Joseph had indeed been talking about Baxter behind his back, but to the police not other gangsters.

'We're nearly there,' soothed Joseph when once more Baxter turned his head to check the cars behind them.

Baxter was still wired tight. 'Just don't fuck up tonight, Joseph, that's all, or I swear...' He left the threat to Joseph's imagination.

Joseph didn't bother to reply. Instead he slowed the car and took the turn-off Baxter indicated, steering the cab down a long, concrete ramp that led to a clump of warehouses set back from the road. The place was dark, virtually invisible to casual passers-by and seemed completely unoccupied during the night, which made it the perfect location to offload a consignment of drugs. If Joseph could just let the NYPD know the location of the drop, Baxter and his associates would all be looking at very long prison sentences. Trouble was, he had no idea how to get away from Baxter's suspicious gaze even for a moment to make that call to Detective Monroe.

Baxter pointed to a warehouse at the end of the road and urged Joseph towards it. The building had been well chosen, as it couldn't be seen until you were almost on top of it. As Joseph drew near, he realised the drop had already taken place and the breaking up of this enormous consignment had begun. Beneath the bright lights of the warehouse, a dozen men walked backwards and forwards between an assortment of cabs, cars and pick-up trucks carrying boxes of varying sizes. They moved briskly and the breath came out of their mouths in urgent white plumes. Joseph recognised some of the men from the cab firm. Others were hard-looking guys who had to be permanent members of Baxter's crew. Joseph parked the cab amongst the other vehicles and then he noticed a familiar figure moving around outside the warehouse, dressed in his trademark Belstaff jacket. It was Esi Kobena.

Baxter told Joseph, 'Get your ass out there and help. Just do what they tell you.'

Joseph did as he was ordered but not before pausing to pull on a thick coat and gloves. To begin with he was glad of the protection against the biting cold, but after a few moments he began to sweat from the exertion of carrying boxes out of the warehouse to the waiting couriers. Joseph worked silently, obeying the orders of Baxter's men, who had set up tables in the warehouse to pile up a seemingly endless number of brown, cardboard boxes filled with product. Behind them, two large container lorries were parked up, their tailgates down and rear doors gaping. These must have been stolen by the suppliers of the main drop. Joseph guessed they would be wiped clean of any forensic evidence before being abandoned here. They would be all that was left behind once the drugs were distributed. By then the police would be left with nothing more than two hot lorries and a very short paper trail, with an alias at the top of it, for the rental of an old warehouse in a run-down part of town.

'Take this one to the black pick-up then this to the green Chevy,' ordered one of Baxter's men.

Joseph silently complied. As he worked, he took in the scene around him, searching for an opportunity to break away, but Baxter's men had the place sewn up tight. Baxter stood to one side, watching the activity and occasionally received whispered updates from his lieutenants. TJ was nowhere to be seen. He obviously didn't want to get his hands dirty, leaving all the risk to Baxter, while he took the lion's share of the reward. Joseph wondered how his second-in-command felt about that.

As the night wore on, the sheer size of the haul astonished Joseph. At one point he overheard one of Baxter's men reveal its contents in an awestruck, over-loud whisper. 'We got it all, man, everything, the whole fucking lot; H, Blow, Roofies, E's, Crystal Meth and GHB. Shit there's even boxes of Viagra, in case you can't get a chubby afterwards.'

One of his friends laughed and Baxter exploded at them for not taking the situation seriously enough. Both men were made to stop supervising the work and haul boxes themselves. Baxter followed them out to make sure there was no slacking. The other men in Baxter's crew took a renewed interest in the job in hand. Some started hulking boxes themselves, others made sure that the nearest civilian stepped up the pace.

Joseph suddenly realised this was his chance. He waited till Baxter had left the warehouse with the offending men and turned towards the back of the building, searching for an exit. All he had to do was get clear enough to run away without being shot at, then he could call Detective Monroe and this nightmare would all be over. He wondered if Baxter would turn states evidence against TJ if it came down to it. Why not if the only alternative was a thirty-stretch? Joseph knew there was no honour in this game. The stakes were too high. He walked slowly to avoid suspicion but was soon free of the main loading bay. In the dark, unlit recess to the rear of the warehouse he could just make out a shadow that looked as if it might be a door and he made for it. No one stopped him, they were all too preoccupied with the task in hand. There were twenty yards between Joseph and the door. Each step took him nearer to freedom. His heart began to pound. He was so close now.

'Where the fuck you think you're going?' boomed Baxter from behind him.

Joseph froze, took a breath and turned to face him. 'I need a piss.'

'Fuck you, wait till it's over!' ordered Baxter, his face contorted with rage as he jabbed a finger at Joseph.

'Okay, okay.' Joseph went straight back to his station and lugged another box. He knew he had hesitated too long and now he'd just blown his best and probably only chance to stop this huge load of drugs from hitting the streets.

Joseph lugged three more boxes. Would this shipment never end? It had to have a street value of millions. No wonder TJ and Baxter were so nervous.

Baxter walked over to him then. He was holding a phone and he looked murderous. 'TJ wants you,' he snarled and handed Joseph the phone.

Joseph took it gingerly and waited to see if Baxter would leave him in peace. Baxter had no such intention. He didn't move and he never let his eyes leave Joseph's. In that moment, Joseph was more convinced than ever before that Baxter wanted to kill him, would have taken immense pleasure from the act in fact.

'Joseph, that you?' asked TJ.

'Yes.'

'Baxter still hanging around? Can he hear you right now?'

Was it just Joseph's imagination or could

Baxter sense he was being talked about. His eyes seemed to narrow at the mention of his name. Joseph told himself to stop acting like an idiot. There was no way Baxter could hear TJ's words. He just had to make sure he didn't do anything dumb like betray the content of the conversation.

'Yes,' said Joseph again, not wishing to elaborate.

'You listen to me, here's what you're going to do. You're gonna tell Baxter I got a special job for you and you got to go right now, you hear?'

'Sure.' Joseph couldn't believe his luck. TJ was going to be his way out of here.

'Then you're gonna come and see me, straightaway, at my house. You got that?'

'Yeah.' Joseph's heart sank. Why would TJ want Joseph to break away from the shipment and come out to his house? What kind of trap was he setting?

'Good.' TJ gave Joseph an address. It wasn't a cheap neighbourhood. Joseph wondered if any of TJ's neighbours knew what he actually did for a living. 'Tell Baxter you got to go now and Joseph...'

'What?'

'Be cool.' Then TJ hung-up.

Joseph handed back the phone and Baxter asked, 'What's he want?'

'He says I've got to go, got a special job for me.'

'Right now?' Joseph could tell Baxter was uncomfortable at that notion. He glanced at the unfinished work going on around him. 'What kind of job?'

'He didn't say.' Why would he on a cell phone, thought Joseph, but he wasn't going to risk enraging Baxter by saying that.

Baxter nodded slowly, as if he sensed betrayal. He looked venomous, like a man who has just caught his wife blowing his best friend. 'You'd better fuck off then,' and he jerked his head in the direction of Joseph's cab.

Joseph said nothing. Instead he just walked slowly towards it wondering how he was ever going to get away from such an incriminating scene while Baxter was still unloading the drugs. Baxter didn't trust Joseph and they both knew it. Was he really going to let Joseph climb into his cab and drive off? It seemed unlikely and he half expected to hear a gun being cocked behind him. Joseph was just waiting for the bullet.

Instead, to his utter astonishment, he reached the safety of his cab and climbed straight in without looking back. As he drove slowly away, he stole a quick, sidelong glance out of the driver's window. Baxter was still standing there, staring straight at him.

Joseph threw the cab up the ramp and left the warehouse behind him. At the same time he found Eddie's number on the speed dial and pressed it. As it started to ring, he hit the speaker option and dropped the phone into his lap so he could watch the road again. He could hear the low chirp of the phone as it dialled Eddie's home. The sound was incessant and the phone rang and rang. Joseph realised Eddie wasn't going to pick up and he cursed his luck. Where the hell was the old man on a night like this? He barely went out of the apartment these days and he picks tonight to visit relatives. Suddenly the ring tone stopped.

'Hello,' said a groggy voice.

'Eddie, thank god, I thought you were out.'

'I was sleeping.'

'Well you got to wake up, my friend. The drop is in and Baxter's men are crawling all over it right now. We got to move fast. Get a pen and paper and I'll give you the address of a warehouse. I want you to call Detective Monroe and tell him to get down there now with plenty of back-up and I mean plenty. Tell him this bust will make him look like a regular Don Johnson. They'll make him Police Commissioner if he doesn't fuck it up. Tell him it's an early Christmas present from me and remind him not to forget his side of our bargain. I want Cyrus out of jail once this is over.'

'Shit, right, okay. You can count on it. What's the address?'

'Just a moment, there's one more thing. I'm on my way to TJ's house right now.'

'What the fuck you playing at, Joseph? Don't go trying to be the hero. Leave it to the cops. You ain't a one-man army.'

'It's not what you think. He called me up, asked me to come over and do a special job. He's got someone or something that needs a ride.'

There was such a long pause on the line, Joseph thought he'd lost the signal. 'You sure about that, Joseph?' asked Eddie finally. 'What if he just wants to get rid of a guy he doesn't trust and he tries to whack you? What are you going to do then?'

'I've thought about that. He wouldn't invite me to his home if he was going to kill me. It'd be somewhere remote, some place he has no links with.'

'Maybe, but it's still a risk. These drug guys don't always think straight. You sure it's worth it? Let's just get Monroe to bust Baxter and his whole crew, they'll soon rat out TJ when they know they ain't got a choice and this will all be over.'

'What if Baxter doesn't rat? We'll have a whole load of drugs and Baxter and his foot soldiers will be locked away, but there's no obvious link to Tina Ferreira's murder. I want this whole thing wrapped up. Sorry,

Eddie but I've got to do this my way.'

'Okay, you're the boss on this one. You gonna give me that address now, or do I have to guess it?'

'Sure, then ring Monroe but get off the line as soon as you can. When I reach TJ's I'll call you back. Don't say anything, just listen in and I'll put us on speakerphone. Do you think you can record us on that fancy sound system of yours?'

'Piece of cake,' said the old man.

'Good, you got that pen ready?'

Joseph took as long as he could to get to TJ's home. He was already waiting for Joseph outside his apartment block. Despite the sub-zero temperature, he was standing on the pavement, dressed in a long, black overcoat, scarf and leather gloves and he was clutching an expensive leather holdall. Joseph had already dialled Eddie's number again and, to his immense relief, the old man answered and stayed silent. Joseph placed his cell phone on the passenger seat and half covered it with a scarf.

'What kept you?' asked TJ.

'What's the job, boss?'

'The job is me.' He climbed into the back of Joseph's cab. 'You're taking me to JFK right now. I got a Delta Airlines flight to Santa Domingo and I'm getting the fuck out. Don't worry, Joseph, you'll be looked after, just get me to JFK as quick as you like.'

'You're leaving now? But the shipment's only just arrived.'

'I already sold my end. Made more money than I could ever spend and believe me I like to spend. When Baxter wakes up in the morning he's gonna find he has a new boss. Mikey Junior Patroni, you remember him, don't you?'

Joseph certainly did. So that was what his trip to New Jersey had been all about. According to Eddie, the Cosa Nostra would never die, they'd just be driven further underground, looking for new and more-ingenious ways to make their dirty money. It sounded as if somebody serious in the Italian–American community had been watching the South Bronx drug trade with covetous eyes. Years ago they'd have taken a man like TJ out without even thinking about it. He would have ended up face down in the Hudson and the Italians would have taken over his whole operation. Times had certainly changed. Now they just bought him out without a shot being fired. It might cost a lot more but no one would be sent away on racketeering charges or a murder rap. How very twenty-first century. It was all so corporate, thought Joseph, the flip side of the capitalist American dream.

'Baxter going to be happy about that, is he?'

'I don't give a shit if he's happy or not. That's business. I know what you're thinking, Joseph. Baxter's been with me right from the start and I gave him every chance.' Joseph wondered why he felt the sudden need to justify his actions. It seemed even a scum-sucking lowlife like TJ needed the world to understand him. It was incredible. 'But he fucked up once too often. You saw that shit about Pinto on the news. Man, they found that motherfucker in a dumpster.' TJ said it with disgust, as if he couldn't believe his second-in-command had been so inept. 'When a man is supposed to disappear, he is meant to disappear, you know what I'm saying. It won't be too long before Baxter fucks up big style, gets us all sent down for life and that means you, too. You think about that, Joseph before you feel too sorry for Baxter. He ain't no friend of yours, neither, kept telling me how we should kill you on account of how you looked like a cop.' TJ sniggered. 'That coked-up fuck is so paranoid he thinks everyone's a cop. I told him, "if Joseph's a cop than Maritza's a fucking Charlie's Angel and I'm Bosley!"' He laughed. 'Men like Baxter, they don't know what they got till they lost it and they're sitting in a cell staring at the walls and wondering what hit them.' The words stung Joseph. TJ could have been describing Cyrus, the man who would pay most for the huge deal he had just done with the Italians. 'He ain't like you and me, Joseph. Now you smart, you know how to do what you're told and keep your mouth closed and I respect that, which is why you doing this job for me.' TJ reached into his inside coat pocket and, for a second, Joseph thought he was going to pull a gun. Instead he brought out a large brown envelope, so big that the coat must have been specially altered to carry such things. 'Know what this is? It's twenty large, Joseph, and it's yours, easiest money you ever earned. All you got to do is get me to the airport and keep your fucking mouth shut afterwards.'

Joseph had to lower his head to hide his feelings. The rage, anger and hurt he had bottled up for months threatened to explode right there and then. This country was no different to Nigeria except the people offering the bribes, the payoffs and the hush money weren't actually working for the government, though Eddie would say some of the men behind them were. What had TJ called it? The easiest money you'll ever earn. All he had to do was keep quiet. Don't say a word. Just take the money. How many times had he heard that before? Just take the money, Joseph. Everyone does it. Don't fight the system, don't go running to the authorities, don't try and change things.

This time it's different. This time it's not

your wife we are coming for. Instead you can watch while your friend goes to prison for the rest of his days. I might as well put a bullet in the back of Cyrus's head right now, thought Joseph. And all for what? Twenty thousand dollars?

TJ was oblivious to Joseph's private turmoil. 'When Baxter asks you where I went you tell him you have no idea. You tell him you dropped me at a casino in Atlantic City for a meeting with some Italians and you ain't seen me since, got it? Dumb fuck will think they killed me, 'cos he don't know any other way of doing business. You don't got to worry about Baxter anyhow, he won't be round for long. The Italians won't work with a psycho like him, not if he ain't one of their own. It's all family, family, family with them. You got to be the first cousin of someone just to become a messenger boy for those guys. They won't trust Baxter 'cos I told them I explained he likes to skim off the top, been doing it to me for years. They are gonna find the consignment is just a few boxes light of what I told 'em, so I think he'll have a little explaining to do.'

'But the drugs will all be gone, broken up into dozens of small drops.'

'Don't matter. I just gave them my book. Every name, every ounce, all of it accounted for. Instead of Baxter coming for the money, it'll be some guy in a badly fitting sweat suit with a big gold chain round his neck, a mozzarella sandwich in one hand and a gun in the other. They ain't hard to spot.'

So TJ was selling Baxter down the river because he was unreliable. Of course the real reason was fear. You don't double-cross a man like Baxter and leave him alive, not if you want to enjoy a comfortable retirement without looking over your shoulder every day for the rest of your life. So Baxter had to go. It was the sensible play and Joseph couldn't say he'd exactly be sorry to hear about it when it happened.

'What about Maritza?'

'What about her? Are you trying to fuck her, Joseph? I think you may be. She is a prize piece of ass.'

'Are the Italians taking her over, too?'

'Why not? What else she gonna do? Shit, Joseph, don't tell me she's been talking about this actress stuff to you. You must be trying to fuck her if you have to listen to that. You think Scorsese's gonna be on the phone to her some time soon? What about Tarantino? Maybe he needs a coked-up beeyatch for his next movie. You think he'll pick Maritza?' He laughed out loud at the notion. 'Maritza knows to keep her mouth shut. She knows a little about my pharmaceutical operation and something about my escort business but she don't have the whole picture. She couldn't give the FBI or the

DEA shit. Not really. To tell you the truth, if it wasn't for my bro, it wouldn't matter to me if she lives or dies, but she knows I can reach back across the water any time and make sure she never talks. It's her mouth and her choice. Stop worrying, Joseph, like I said she don't know too much.'

Joseph knew he was taking a big risk but he had to try to get it on tape. 'She knows all about Tina Ferreira.'

TJ exploded. 'What she tell you about that? Damn it!' His face twisted as he tried to compose himself. 'Tina got what she deserved. That fucking ho was screwing Pinto behind my back, telling him all of our business. You think I can let her keep walking and breathing after that? No fucking way.' TJ's temper was up now. 'Maritza can't talk about that to the cops or they'll take her down, too. She put a gun in some sap's cab for me. He gonna take the rap. Who else has Maritza been talking to about fucking Tina, that bitch!'

'No one, just me. She only told me so I'd know not to fuck with you. I told her I'm not so stupid to bite the hand that feeds. She's so scared of you she'd never say a word about Tina to anyone else. I just wanted to know how you felt about it. I was hoping you'd leave her alone.'

'I'll leave her, for now,' muttered TJ, his temper subsiding into ill humour once he accepted the explanation. 'But you remember who owns her, just in case you start to get the notion she's Julia Roberts and you're Richard Gere. It don't work like that in real life. She's the property of the Italians now and don't you forget it. If my bro stills wants her in a couple of years, I'll buy her back for him.'

Joseph wondered how many more girls went over to the Italians in this deal. TJ was even worse than Baxter. Ray Baxter was a bloodthirsty killer, but TJ got others to do his dirty work for him, then he sold them on like slaves and disappeared with the cash. How many victims had there been in TJ's three-year reign as emperor of the South Bronx? How many addicts had overdosed, rival gang members been killed, prostitutes disposed of once they become a liability. Joseph prayed Eddie was getting all this. 'Don't worry I know the score and I won't forget how it works.'

'Where in hell are we?' snapped TJ.

'Close to the Cross Bronx Expressway.'

'I don't recognise this part of town.'

'It's quicker, trust me. It gets us on the main road further down.'

They were passing more vacant lots that had been sidelined for landfill and Joseph made his mind up. He said, 'I go past here all the time. We are right by the lot scheduled for the new recycling centre on

Amsterdam Avenue.' Then he pressed the brake and the car lurched, he pressed it once more and it lurched again. 'Oh shit,' he said.

'What the fuck?' asked TJ.

'I don't believe it. I think the sparks have gone again.' He made the cab bunny-hop along the road by pressing sharply down on the accelerator and lifting his foot off it over and over, sending TJ pitching forwards then back into his seat with each press of the brakes.

'I don't fucking believe this,' shouted TJ.

'I'm sorry, I'll take a look. I can fix it, no problem. I'll just pull over by the new recycling site.' TJ cursed Joseph, his cab and the world in general, though he showed no sign of suspecting it was deliberate.

Unbeknown to TJ, Joseph had just given Eddie their exact location.

Joseph parked the cab by the side of the road, next to a wire fence that ran round the perimeter of the recycling plant. There were "keep-out" signs every few yards even though the land had been completely cleared and there was surely nothing left to steal. Joseph got out of the cab and flipped the bonnet, leaned in and pretended to mess with the spark plugs. Joseph knew he would have to stall TJ for as long as possible but he also knew the man was no idiot. If he had even the slightest suspicion he was being double-crossed he'd gun Joseph down in the street without a second thought.

TJ wound the rear side window down as far as it would go. It was child proofed, so he only had the narrowest of gaps between the glass and the roof of the car to poke his large head through. He barked at Joseph, 'You better fucking fix this heap of shit and I mean quick. I'm running out of patience.'

'Nearly there.'

'I hope so or I'll shoot you and leave you in the gutter, you dumb fuck.' TJ sounded as if he meant it. In a moment he was likely to try and get out of the cab and take a look himself and then there would be hell to pay.

The thought of TJ rumbling what was really going on was a stress Joseph could do without and he prayed that Eddie had heard their location clearly on the phone and had taken the appropriate action. Joseph could hear him swearing and shouting in the back of the cab as his frustration began to boil over. Where in hell were the cops when you needed them? Got to keep TJ in the car.

Joseph walked back round to TJ's window in a bid to placate him. 'I'm sorry, Mr Jakes,' he said, 'damn sparks have played up before, but I know I can get us going in just a moment.'

TJ froze then. He raised his head, eyed Joseph suspiciously and gave his driver a murderous look. It was as if he had just really noticed Joseph for the first time.

'What?' asked Joseph innocently.

'How'd you know my name?' demanded TJ, in a quiet voice that was like ice.

Before Joseph could answer, TJ started to rummage in his jacket and this time he wasn't looking for the envelope. 'Nobody on the street knows my name, which makes you a...'

At that exact moment, the first siren sounded in the distance behind them. Joseph had longed for that sound, but this was not an ideal time for him and he didn't hang around long enough for TJ to finish his sentence and call him a cop.

TJ tried to open the door with his left hand and, at exactly the same moment, he used his right to draw a gun and fire in one fluid movement. The bullet from his automatic missed Joseph by inches as it passed harmlessly over his head. Joseph had dived low, moving backwards and to the side at just the right instance but he bounced off the opened driver's door, landing awkwardly, half in and half out of the cab, ending up face down on the front seat. By now TJ had realised he could not open his door, which was centrally locked, and he howled in frustration. The sound of the sirens had multiplied and they were getting louder and louder.

With Joseph still off balance, TJ made his

decisive move. He sat up in his seat, leaned forwards and held his gun high, angling the nose of the pistol downwards so it pointed through the glass partition. Joseph rolled round in the driver's seat in a desperate effort to get free, but he was hampered by the enclosed space. The blast from the gun had made his ears ring, almost deafening him, and he was disorientated. TJ had moved quickest and, when Joseph's head came round, he found he was staring straight up into the barrel of the gun. There was no way he could dodge a bullet from there. TJ simply couldn't miss. It was all over. A sick gleam of satisfaction filled the gangster's eyes and he pulled the trigger. TJ fired and the cab was filled with noise and smoke.

15

The partition of the cab took the full force of the bullet at point-blank range but, incredibly, when the smoke cleared, Joseph realised the glass was unbroken. The partition was scorched by the gunfire and there was a hole where the bullet had impacted against the first layer of glass but miraculously the second layer had held. TJ's face was now obscured by a squat shape that looked like a jelly fish with a flattened, embedded bullet at its heart.

Joseph needed no further urging. He rolled out of the cab. TJ belatedly realised the screen was bulletproof but, as soon as he hit the ground, Joseph bounced back up to his feet and ran. Behind him he could hear TJ shouting as the gangster tried to barge the door open. As Joseph ran, there was a further single shot and the rear side window smashed into a thousand tiny shards that spread out all over the ground like snow-flakes. Joseph glanced back over his shoulder in time to see TJ struggling to force his burly frame through the broken window. As he did so, four police cars, two unmarked and two squad cars, screeched to a halt around the cab. One of them was still moving as armed officers bounced from the vehicles.

The policemen were still some way from TJ but they fanned out round the damaged window and trained their guns on him. He was half out of the car, like a cork that's stuck in a bottle, when one of the officers shouted, 'Freeze!'

His colleagues followed the officer's lead and there were cries of 'drop it' and 'put the fucking gun down now!'

TJ immediately dropped his gun but then he ducked back into the cab. The armed men of the NYPD were prepared for most things but not that. TJ disappearing back into the cab stopped them in their tracks and gave them a dilemma. All of a sudden, the officers didn't know what to do. TJ had surrendered his weapon but it was always possible he had a back-up piece. They advanced very slowly and with supreme caution and the officer at the front again took the lead. 'Stay in the fucking cab!' he screamed. 'Put your hands where we can fucking see them! Do it now.' But TJ just ignored them. He wasn't even moving, just sitting quietly in the middle of the rear seat.

Joseph had stopped running as soon as he saw the police cars arrive and he had a better view than the police. He could see TJ through the front windshield. He was partly obscured by the damaged half of the partition window, but Joseph could still clearly make out the raised right arm and the mobile phone. Joseph moved round the front of the car to get a better look and was shocked to see how calm TJ appeared. Just before he hung up the phone, a beatific smile crossed the man's face. Joseph walked quickly back to his cab.

As soon as he had made his call, TJ started to obey police instructions. With exaggerated caution, he put up his hands. One of the officers trained his gun on TJ at close range while another opened the door from the outside. TJ then eased himself out of the cab. As soon as he was standing on the street, a trio of officers pounced on him, turned TJ round, spread his palms out on the roof of the cab and patted him down. When they were sure he was clean, the officers spun him back round to face a new arrival. Assistant Chief McCavity wanted to make this arrest personally. At her side was Detective Monroe, looking pretty pleased with himself. It seemed he was McCavity's new favourite. There was no sign of Detective Baker. Clever lad, thought Joseph, let your boss take the credit and hang onto her coat tails while she flies onwards and upwards.

McCavity read TJ his rights and he just grinned at her. 'Fuck you,' he said. 'You got nothing.'

Joseph reached into his cab and retrieved his mobile phone. 'You still there, Eddie,' he asked while TJ looked on in something like amazement.

'That you, Joseph? You okay? I heard the shots and...'

'I'm good, not a scratch, thanks to a bullet-proof partition. Glad you stayed on the line though. Did you get it all?' asked Joseph down the line.

'Every word, my friend,' replied Eddie.

Joseph looked into TJ's eyes and felt nothing more than pure hatred for this drug-dealing, murderous bastard. The one thing that stopped him from punching the gangster to the ground was the satisfaction of knowing that TJ would soon be looking at thirty long years in the can. 'Sorry, TJ,' he said and he nodded towards McCavity. 'Apparently she's got everything and all of it on tape.' He held the mobile phone up for TJ to see.

The lopsided smirk vanished and the cocky attitude faded away. It took a second for TJ to realise what Joseph had done to him but when it finally sunk in that he had been double-crossed and was doomed to spend the rest of his life behind bars, he screamed, 'You son-of-a-whore!' and lunged at Joseph. Thankfully he was already in handcuffs and the three burly officers simply tripped him then planted him face-first on the ground till his rage burned out. He looked like a small, helpless child having a tantrum. The burliest officer even sat on him for good measure. 'I'll fucking kill you, you fucking cocksucker, I'll kill you, I'll kill you...' TJ shouted it over and over again until he could barely breathe from the effort required to continue the tirade.

'No, you won't,' said McCavity calmly, 'you're going to a very small cell in a maximum-security unit in a nice new state penitentiary that no one has ever escaped from and you'll be in there until you're a very old man, that's what you are going to do. I'll be sipping chilled orange juice on the porch of my sunny little retirement home in Florida and you'll still be eating shifty prison food and taking it up the ass from some Puerto Rican with a long memory and a liking for black meat.' McCavity pointed at Joseph. 'If I was you, I'd kill myself not him.' She walked calmly away from TJ.

Her outburst was so unexpected it stopped the man in his tracks. As McCavity's figure receded, TJ called after her desperately. 'I'll make a deal!' he screamed. 'I'll tell you everything!'

'Mister, you ain't got anything I want,' she said simply.

TJ must have realised what his future held then. When they finally led him away, he was weeping.

With TJ out of the way, Joseph suddenly remembered something. He got back on his mobile phone and asked, 'You still there, Eddie?'

'Of course I am. You think I'd want to miss any of this?'

'Just before they got him out of the cab, TJ made a call. Did you hear who he was talking to?'

'No, I couldn't make much of that out. He was speaking too low. All I heard was part of an address, if that's any use to you?'

'What was it?'

'Morris Heights,' said Eddie, and Joseph finally realised what TJ was up to.

'I'll call you later,' he said and hung up. He was already running back towards McCavity and Monroe. When they turned to face him, Joseph said, 'Your key witness is in danger. Come with me now or you'll have another body on your hands.'

It didn't take much persuasion to get McCavity and Monroe to divert some of their resources towards Morris Heights. Detectives escorted TJ back to the precinct in one unmarked car while the two remaining squad cars followed McCavity's car, whose driver was being urged to abandon all caution by Joseph. There was no need for stealth, so it was flashing lights and sirens all the way. McCavity and Monroe might not have cared much for the fate of a drugged-up moll, but Joseph made sure they never lost sight of Maritza's value as a witness. She had seen much of the evil of TJ's empire from a front-row seat. Joseph had already proved himself to Monroe and, since she had just managed to arrest the drug dealer who had eluded her detectives these past three years, McCavity was becoming a late convert to his way of thinking.

Joseph dialled Maritza's number. He prayed she would answer from anywhere but home. Maybe she was out and whoever

TJ was sending to silence her would be left standing harmlessly outside on the landing until the cops arrived to arrest him.

The phone rang four times then a woman's voice said, 'Hello.'

'Maritza? Is that you?' asked Joseph.

'Yeah, who is...' She must have finally put the voice to a name. 'That you, Joseph?' she asked, sounding surprised.

'Listen to me, Maritza, there's no time, you got to get out. You've got to get out of there, you hear?'

'Get out? What do you mean?'

'TJ's sending someone over. He's gonna kill you if you don't leave now.'

'TJ? No, why would he do...'

'The cops picked him up and he's worried you'll tell them everything about Tina. He knows he's got to shut you up, Maritza, for good.'

'He wouldn't...'

'Yes, he would, Maritza. Look what happened to Tina.'

'No, he...' She was unsure but he could tell from the wavering in her voice that she was scared. 'He wouldn't...'

'Maritza, you've got to go now.' Before he could say anything further there was a loud banging on the line and she screamed. 'What was that?' asked Joseph.

'The door,' she said, sounding terrified now. 'Someone trying to get in.'

'Don't answer it, whatever you do, don't answer it. Find some place to hide. You can do that, Maritza, find some place to hide.' Even as he said it, he realised how futile it was going to be. Whoever was out there, the front door would be no obstacle for them. It would only hold for a moment and there was nowhere for Maritza to hide in that little place. Did he think they wouldn't look under the bed or in her wardrobe and, if she locked herself in the bathroom, it would only delay the inevitable for a few seconds. If they were going to gun her down in the apartment, she'd be dead long before they could reach her. Maritza was silent, she must have gone into shock. 'Maritza, do you hear me?'

Just then there was an even bigger crash and Maritza screamed once more, louder than before. A loud but muffled male voice shouted, 'Shut up, bitch!' They'd broken the door down. They were in the apartment. Maritza must have dropped the phone or, more likely, had it wrenched from her hand and seen it smashed against a wall, because the line went dead.

Joseph leaned forwards urgently and started giving directions to the police driver, telling him which route he should take. The driver turned to McCavity for her permission and she simply said, 'Go ahead.'

The police driver knew what he was

doing. He'd had training and he was good. When Joseph diverted him along the lesser-known side streets, he manoeuvred the car expertly. A number of times, Joseph thought he'd lost it, with the back end of the car threatening to give way and send them into a spin but each time he instantly regained control and the car shot round a corner, before resuming its journey. As they drove, Detective Monroe gave Joseph an excited commentary on the events at the warehouse. 'It was just like you said it would be, Joseph. We caught a whole heap of guys loading boxes into cabs and pick-ups. They thought the warehouse was an ideal location because you couldn't see it from the road but it all backfired on them because there was no way out of there except by coming up that big, concrete ramp, unless they were looking to jump into the river. In this weather I reckon they'd last about a minute before dying of hypothermia. Anyway, we came crashing down that ramp with a double SWAT team and half the NYPD. They just put up their hands and gave up, not that they had a choice. I have never seen such a huge consignment before. I tell you, the DEA are going to be eating out of our hands after this bust.'

'Did you get everybody?' asked Joseph. He wasn't too interested in a lurid account of the arrests just now. 'Did you get a mean-looking, skinny guy with dreadlocks called Ray Baxter?'

'Sorry, no one by that name or description,' confirmed Monroe.

Joseph would have put money on Baxter getting away. He must have a sixth sense for danger. How had he known to leave before the police got there? Did he just not trust Joseph enough to hang around once TJ had summoned him? 'Then I've got a good idea where he is right now,' said Joseph. He knew his worst suspicions had been confirmed.

The three cars careered round the corner in a line and into Maritza's street. They pulled up in the middle of the road by Maritza's building, forming an uneven blockade by the steps to her apartment. The officers were about to leap from the lead car when Joseph spotted a distinctive black BMW pulling away a few yards from them.

'Wait, not yet. That looks like Baxter's car. If she ain't dead, she's in there!' The driver needed no further orders. He gunned the squad car towards the BMW and shot off after it. Baxter probably wasn't expecting an unmarked police car to come screaming after him and he hadn't been trained as a driver. Before Baxter reached the end of the street the police car had made up ground and was level with the BMW occupying the opposite lane. Baxter was driving with

Kobena in the passenger seat next to him. Both men turned their gaze to the police car alongside them and when Baxter saw Joseph his mouth fell open.

Baxter started to reach for a gun but the police driver was having none of it. He slammed their car sideways and it gave the BMW a sturdy, glancing blow sending it careering off the road. It ploughed across a pavement and through some iron railings. McCavity's driver performed an elegant handbrake turn and the car did a one-eighty and ended up pointing back at the wrecked BMW.

Baxter looked stunned as he dragged himself out of the car, clutching his gun. He had blood on his forehead and was dragging an injured leg after him. The last thing Joseph would remember of Baxter was the look of sheer rage on the man's face as he realised he was trapped. Officers from the two other squad cars had already pulled up at the scene and emerged from their vehicles with guns drawn, pointing them straight at Baxter. He managed a disoriented stagger towards them and tried to raise his gun. There was one last shouted warning for Baxter to drop the gun but the words were inaudible because, at that same moment, Baxter tried to fire and he was cut down with a volley of shots from a number of weapons. It was like a firing squad. Baxter's head jerked back, his feet were lifted off the ground and he was knocked backwards from the force of multiple bullets. Joseph guessed he was dead before his head hit the floor.

A moment later, Kobena stepped slowly from the wreck, took in the spectacle of his boss's dead body lying in the street and gave up without a fight. Joseph ran to the car, popped the trunk and there was Maritza, lying motionless, face up and eyes closed. Joseph thought he was too late, but a medic who had been travelling with the police squad pushed him roughly to one side, scooping Maritza up and lifting her out of the trunk. He lay the prone woman on the ground and felt for vital signs, then got to work on reviving her. 'She's alive,' was all he offered but the words were music to Joseph's ears.

Moments later, Maritza gasped, opened her eyes and sat straight up. When they'd calmed her down, an officer explained what had happened and she was coaxed towards an ambulance that had been called before she regained consciousness. As she was led silently away, Maritza glanced over at Joseph and they exchanged a look. He did not expect any thanks from her, nor did he receive any. It was enough that she was still alive.

Detective Monroe came up to him then

and shook Joseph's hand warmly. 'Thanks, Joseph,' he said, 'it all went down exactly as you said it would.'

'Don't forget to go and see Eddie about the tapes. He's got it all, everything is on the tapes.'

'I'll go there right now. I'll drop you home at the same time if you like.' He looked a little embarrassed. 'I'm afraid we can't let you have your cab back just yet. The forensic boys will be all over it for while.'

'I understand. In that case a ride home would be good.'

Joseph didn't notice McCavity as she walked up behind him, then he felt a hand against his back. 'You did good tonight, Mr Solinka.' She patted him on the shoulder. 'Real good.'

As she walked away, Joseph wondered if she had deliberately mispronounced his name to remind him of his true place at the bottom of the food chain, or if she really was that damn ignorant. He would never know for sure.

EPILOGUE

Cyrus sat awkwardly on the sofa as if he had forgotten what comfort felt like. Eddie was there, too, cheerfully heckling politicians on the evening news, while Joseph cleared away their empty coffee cups.

'I can't believe how quick they let you go,' the old man told Cyrus.

'I know.' Cyrus nodded as if he could not quite fully believe his good fortune.

'I'm sure it has nothing to do with the fact their key witness was caught red-handed in Baxter's crashed car with Maritza in the trunk,' answered Joseph, and Eddie chuckled to himself at the thought of McCavity's embarrassment. Joseph continued, 'I spoke to Monroe. They could make Cyrus's life difficult, since he confessed to working for Baxter a couple of times, but they know he is low-level. They arrested the wrong man and now they got the real deal with TJ so why keep Cyrus?'

'How is the girl?' asked Eddie.

'Okay, apart from a crack on the head. I think she's only alive today because Baxter knows he fucked up when he failed to make Pinto disappear. He would have killed

Maritza in her apartment and just left her there but TJ likes his dirty work tidied up, which it would have been if we'd arrived about half a minute later.'

'You think she'll testify?'

'Monroe thinks so. Baxter's dead, TJ's behind bars and she knows he tried to kill her. They can always threaten her with a vice bust and they have TJ on tape saying she planted the gun on Cyrus, so I don't think she has a lot of choice. It's the only sensible play.'

'Did they get Baxter's whole crew?'

'So they say, along with a group of corrupt drivers.'

'Putting an end to New York's first and only pharmaceutical taxi service,' announced Eddie. 'Cyrus, I cannot decide if you are the dumbest man in New York or the luckiest, which is it?'

'Both, I guess,' conceded Cyrus.

'Now Baxter's dead everybody is queuing up to rat out TJ in return for a reduced sentence,' Joseph continued, 'the cops think they'll be able to retrieve most of the drugs, taking out the dealers in the process.'

'And TJ?' asked Eddie.

'It don't look good for him. TJ is implicated in the murders of Tina Ferreira and Eduardo Pinto, the kidnapping of Maritza and the heading up of a drugs operation with a near-record level of product. Monroe thinks he's a cert for life, with no prospect of parole.'

'That motherless fuck. The amount of misery he's caused other people, I got no sympathy. Let him take his medicine,' said Eddie. 'And I wouldn't want to be the boss of that New Jersey crew who just paid top dollar for a cartel that got busted up the same night. You think Tony Soprano would get away with that?'

'I doubt if Mikey Junior's got much of a future,' admitted Joseph.

'So that's it then, the whole thing's wrapped up just like you wanted,' said the old man.

'As good as.'

Eddie went back to watching the news but then he said, 'You know it was a good job that cab you bought was fitted with bullet-proof glass.'

'Yeah, the guy I bought it from must have done it after TJ's brother murdered those drivers. Kind of ironic when you think about it.'

Eddie's mouth fell open. 'Must have? You mean you didn't know it was there?'

'He never mentioned it to me.'

'Jeez, so back then, when TJ fired his gun at you, you must have thought...'

Joseph put up a hand. 'Don't even go there.'

He was saved from discussing his good

fortune further when a key turned in the lock. It was Yomi back from school. He beamed when he realised Cyrus was free and hugged his father's oldest friend, then he high-fived Eddie. Suddenly a familiar face appeared on the TV

'Oh look,' said Eddie. 'It's Robocop.'

Assistant Chief McCavity had just walked out from behind a hastily erected screen. Detective Monroe was at her side, sharing the limelight, while the Commissioner watched them both with the silent approval of a parent.

McCavity was in her element. You could tell she just loved a good press conference. Her normal shabby day-wear had been replaced by the kind of expensive, designer suit that only got trotted out for the media and she had just had her hair fixed. She wore her most solemn look, on a face she probably reserved for funerals or announcements of great magnitude. This was clearly going to be the latter.

'I would like to make a short statement,' she began. 'As you know, the murder of Tina Ferreira led to one of the most intensive investigations in the history of the 41st precinct. I promised you then that we would not rest until her killer was behind bars. We questioned dozens of witnesses and potential suspects. We also received assistance from a large number of right-minded members of the South Bronx public, true citizens of this country who are as sickened by the gun crime in New York as we are.'

'I think she means you, Joseph,' said Eddie dryly.

'The man hours spent on this case were incalculable but far from wasted. Our investigations took a new turn when we linked Tina's killer to a major drug-dealing operation. I am proud to say that last night we took down an international crime syndicate based here in the heart of the South Bronx, seizing a haul of drugs, the like and size of which has rarely been seen on the eastern seaboard. I would like to pay tribute to my team of dedicated officers, who worked tirelessly to bring this case to a conclusion. It was good old-fashioned police work that brought us this result, nothing more, nothing less.'

She nodded emphatically in case there were any simpletons watching who didn't understand what she was telling them. 'A number of highly dangerous individuals have been removed from the streets of New York. I am confident we will see them charged in relation to serious drugs offences, money laundering, racketeering and, yes, murder.'

'Oh, she's good, I'll give her that,' said Eddie. 'What a showman! PT Barnum got nothing on her.'

'I am convinced that the South Bronx is a safer place today than it was just twenty-four hours ago. As our investigations are still ongoing however, I am unable to answer any of your questions at this time.'

'Meaning we got to have another press conference tomorrow and I get to wear my fancy suit again.' Eddie was shaking his head in wonderment at McCavity's cheek.

'I thank you for your patience and I will leave you with a quote from Lois Bujold, who said "The dead cannot cry out for justice; it is a duty of the living to do so for them." Thank you.' McCavity rose and left the table, leaving the assembled journalists to take the bait and call their excited questions after her retreating figure as it disappeared behind the screen. It only served to make her appear an even more remote and important figure. Like every good cabaret act, McCavity knew exactly when to leave the stage and leave her audience crying out for more.

'There goes the next mayor of New York,' said Eddie in something resembling grudging admiration. 'Throw that woman in a sewer and she'd come up covered in maple syrup. Shame she forgot to mention your name, though.'

'Oh, I don't know,' said Joseph. 'That kind of fame I could do without.'

'Maybe you got a point there. The residents of Highbridge might get a little nervous if they learn they are living next door to a gangbuster. Still it pisses me off she's gonna get a promotion when she had the wrong guy in the can before you showed up and solved the case for her.'

'Eddie, a very wise man once told me that the world stinks and the sooner I got used to it the easier it would be.'

Eddie laughed, 'I'd say he had a point, your friend. He must have been a real clever guy.'

'Plus, there are some people in New Jersey who aren't too happy right now. I'd rather they blame McCavity than me.' Then he added, 'Anyway we'd better be going.'

'We?' asked Eddie. 'I thought I was sitting Yomi,' and the boy seemed just as puzzled.

'Sorry, did I give you that impression?'

'You sure did,' said the old man.

'Then I apologise. No, you and Cyrus and Yomi and me are all going out tonight.'

'How come?' asked Eddie, who seemed a little put out at not being consulted.

'On account of the small financial reward the NYPD is bestowing on me for performing my civic duty.'

'A reward!' cried Yomi.

'Don't get excited, son, it isn't that much.' Of course it was just another bribe of sorts. Joseph would receive the money in return for the unspoken understanding that he would not go rushing to the newspapers with his side of the story. McCavity could then continue her unstoppable rise to the top. Joseph didn't really mind. Besides, a commendation letter from the NYPD might come in handy the next time he applied to join them. Till then it was back to riding round in a cab all day.

'So where are we going?' asked Eddie impatiently.

Joseph reached into his inside pocket and pulled out four tickets. 'Just the Yankee stadium. I hear they are playing some guys called the Red Sox?' he asked doubtfully.

'Yes!' cried Yomi and he rolled over onto his back, threw both arms up and started punching the air. 'Dad, you're the best!'

'Eddie, this is the least I could do after all your help.'

'If you put it like that, count me in,' said Eddie. 'Those Yankees gonna kick butt tonight eh, Yomi?'

'Definitely!'

'Then let's move,' said Joseph.

Yomi went to fetch his Yankees' cap and the others gathered up their hats and coats. Joseph wasn't entirely sure why he had spent so much money on baseball tickets but he suspected it had quite a lot to do with staring down the barrel of an automatic, fully expecting to die. He had been given a timely reminder that life was short and always hangs by the thinnest of threads.

Cyrus seemed forlorn. 'I should be paying for those tickets,' he told Joseph glumly. 'You saved my life and now you are buying baseball tickets. I don't know how I'm ever gonna repay you.'

'I didn't really buy them, the NYPD did and I reckon they owe you a night at the game. Besides there is something I would like from you.'

'Anything, Joseph,' said Cyrus solemnly and he placed his hand on Joseph's shoulder. 'Just name it.'

'Four chilli dogs.'

'What?'

'At the stadium tonight.'

'Is that all?'

'Chilli dogs ain't cheap at the Yankee stadium, Cyrus. I reckon that should make us evens.'

Cyrus tried to speak his gratitude but instead he blinked and wiped his eyes with the back of his hand.

Joseph embraced him. 'You are free, my friend, and that's all that matters.'

The awkward moment was broken when Yomi bounced back into the room wearing his Yankees' cap. Joseph picked up his jacket then ushered everyone to the door. 'You guys go on ahead, I want to speak with Yomi.' He waited until Eddie and Cyrus were out of earshot. 'You realise this is a one-off deal, you are still grounded.'

'I know, Dad, for like five years or something.'

There had already been a long discussion about Joey Neste, and Yomi knew he had let his father down. 'I know you have reached the age when you feel a strong urge to defy your father. I felt it, too, all boys do, but I also expected to be punished when he caught me. Do you understand, Yomi? It's my job to keep you from messing up like your friend. I'll trust you again one day but you've got to earn that trust.'

Yomi nodded. 'Okay.'

'Now catch up Uncle Eddie and Uncle Cyrus while I lock the door,' and Joseph watched while Yomi ran after the two proxy uncles from his dysfunctional American family.

Suddenly Yomi stopped and turned back to his father. 'Dad?' He was walking backwards as he spoke. 'You do know who the Boston Red Sox are, don't you?'

'Let's see.' Joseph pretended to think for a moment. 'I get so confused. Are they the ones who recorded that song about a hump. You know...' and he pretended to do a little dance in the corridor. 'My hump, my hump...'

'Dad! That was the Black-Eyed Peas! You know, really.' Yomi was still laughing when he caught up with Eddie and Cyrus.

Joseph locked up the apartment and walked down the corridor after his son. Yomi was a good kid. He had a kind heart, he cared about their friends and, with Apara gone, they were probably the only family he was ever going to have now. The boy would need his uncles. Yomi would have to be tough to survive in the projects. If he was going to make it out of there at all he would have to be strong and he'd have to be smart. Most of all, thought Joseph, he would have to be streetwise.

This Large Print Book, for people
who cannot read normal print,
is published under the auspices of

THE ULVERSCROFT FOUNDATION